"I'm ready to move along whenever you are."

The words had no sooner left Carrie's mouth when the sound of a high-powered rifle split the night air and bark and pine needles rained down on them.

"Run!" Thad shouted as he grabbed her hand and took off sprinting through the trees, doing his best not to go too fast for Carrie. He didn't want to end up making her fall or injuring her ankle further, but they needed to put as much distance as they could between them and the shooter. Chastising himself for spending too much time when they stopped to rest, instead of keeping them moving in the direction of the logging road, he turned loose of her hand and slowed down enough for her to pass him. "Get in front of me."

"Why?" she asked even as she jogged around him to take the lead.

"Because if he takes another shot, I want to make sure he misses you," he answered truthfully. If someone was going to be shot, he'd gladly take the bullet to keep her safe.

Kathie Ridings lives in her native southern Illinois on the land her family settled in 1839. A former teacher of tole folk-art painting, basket weaving and crochet, she's always loved to read. Now she plots her books while painting, weaving a basket or crocheting something warm to wear. Readers may contact Kathie by emailing kathieridings@gmail.com or find her on Facebook at Facebook.com/Kathie-Ridings-100209191904884.

Books by Kathie Ridings

Love Inspired Suspense

Wyoming Christmas Peril
Cougar Mountain Ambush

Visit the Author Profile page at LoveInspired.com.

COUGAR MOUNTAIN AMBUSH

KATHIE RIDINGS

LOVE INSPIRED SUSPENSE

INSPIRATIONAL ROMANCE

LOVE INSPIRED® SUSPENSE
INSPIRATIONAL ROMANCE

ISBN-13: 978-1-335-58851-7

PLEASE RECYCLE · THIS PRODUCT IS RECYCLABLE

Recycling programs
for this product may
not exist in your area.

Cougar Mountain Ambush

Love Inspired
22 Adelaide St. West, 41st Floor
Toronto, Ontario M5H 4E3, Canada
www.LoveInspired.com

Printed in U.S.A.

I can do all things through Christ
which strengtheneth me.
—Philippians 4:13

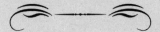

To my sweet Josie and Evie with all my love.

ONE

Wyoming Game and Fish Department conservation officer Carrie Caldwell stopped inputting her impression of Whisper Lake into her electronic tablet to look up at the brilliant blue, late September sky. The sound interrupting her thoughts had to be either the loudest swarm of bees she'd ever heard or someone was flying a drone nearby.

Looking around, she spotted the quadcopter drone hovering about forty feet above the smooth-as-glass surface of the spring-fed mountain lake in front of her. She dismissed it as insignificant. A photographer with a camera mount was probably taking pictures of the panoramic views or capturing images of the abundant wildlife in the area. She didn't have time to worry about it. She was here on the Hanson family's ranch to take water samples and assess the habitat management of their private Cougar Mountain Wildlife Preserve. For all she knew, it could be, and probably was, a member of the Hanson family operating the drone.

If she remembered correctly, she'd been told one of the brothers had left his position as an FBI special agent hostage negotiator to become a nature photographer. He had a reputation for being one of the best, most respected in the entire state.

But while she speculated on who the operator might be, the quadcopter moved closer to hover within ten feet of her, about six feet off the ground. An icy chill raced up her spine and a frightened gasp escaped her suddenly dry throat when she noticed a semiautomatic pistol attached just below the gimbal camera on the drone's undercarriage—pointed directly at her. It was illegal for anyone to arm a drone, but she wasn't naive enough to think that people would hesitate to break the law to serve their own interests.

Keeping her eyes fixed on the drone's deadly weapon, she raised her hands in a gesture of surrender as she started inching backward. Where was she going to go? She'd had to hike two miles up to the lake from where she'd parked her work truck. There was a line of lodgepole pine trees some twenty yards behind her, but the odds of her making it to them before the drone caught up to her or whoever was operating it fired the gun were slim to none. If she could just make it to those trees, the drone wouldn't be able to follow her as easily as out in the open. At least, that's what she hoped.

But for every step back she took, the drone moved forward, keeping pace and making escape impossible. When she took a few steps to the side, the gun mount swiveled to keep the pistol aimed straight at her head until the operator maneuvered the drone directly in front of her again.

It felt like ice water had replaced the blood in her veins. Who could possibly be behind this? And why?

"If this is some kind of prank, I'm not finding it funny," she warned as anger born of fear began to fill her. She hoped the drone had a microphone or that the viewer could read lips. "If you aren't joking and you really are threatening me, it's going to get you arrested. Either way, if you don't cease and desist you're going to be in big trouble with the law, mister."

As a game warden, her jurisdiction wasn't limited to enforcing hunting and fishing laws. She was also a Wyoming peace officer, and as such, had all the authority of any other member of law enforcement. It was against the law to mount a firearm to a drone—and even if it wasn't, it was illegal to threaten any law enforcement officer with a gun. And she had every intention of seeing that charges were brought against whoever was behind this recklessly dangerous stunt.

When she took another step back, her boot came down on a fallen branch, throwing her off balance and painfully rolling her ankle. She fell to the ground in an undignified heap. Before she could get up, the drone came closer, hovering less than three feet from her face. Her heart pounded hard against her ribs as she awaited the machine's next move. If the operator fired the gun now, there was nothing she could do to defend herself. She would be dead and because she was the only warden in the one-person WGFD Eagle Fork station, there was a good chance it could take days, even weeks for her remains to be found. She shuddered.

Due to the numerous predators inhabiting the mountains, her body might *never* be recovered. She didn't want her parents and brothers to go through the anguish of never knowing what had happened to her, never having closure and the comfort of a church service acknowledging her passing because they were holding on to the hope she would one day return to them. *Please, dear Lord, please don't let things end this way. Please help me make it out of this alive so my family doesn't have to go through that.*

Her mind filled with regrets. At the top of the list was her decision to decline Dr. Hanson's offer. He had proposed that she meet him at the Cougar Mountain Wildlife Rehabilitation Center he'd started on the northern side of his family's mountain. His plan had been to give her a tour of the facility, then saddle a couple of his horses for them to ride over to Whisper Valley where the lake was located. But she'd chosen to hike into Whisper Valley alone. She had several lakes and rivers in the area she needed to take samples from for testing, and when she did pay a visit to the rehab operation, she didn't want to rush, the way she'd have to if she combined the water sampling and the tour in one visit. She wanted to take her time at the rehab center, enjoy observing the animals and give his efforts her full attention. Her predecessor, Lyle Markham, had talked extensively about Dr. Hanson's ideas and innovative techniques of rehabilitating wildlife to be released back into the wild, and she looked forward to seeing it for herself.

But she'd never get that chance now. And because she'd turned down the doctor's offer, she didn't have him there with her to witness this attempt to intimidate or even kill her.

She shook her head in disgust. It was ridiculous to be held hostage by a plastic machine. Deciding enough was enough, she started to get up. But the drone swooped in even closer and she had to lean back on her elbows to keep from being hit in the face by one of the propellers.

Anger, hot and swift, coursed through her as she glared up at her tormentor. "Why are you doing this?" she demanded, her nerves so tight she was certain they would snap at any moment. "What do you want from me? If you're going to shoot me, then stop taunting me. Just do it and get it over with!"

She'd no sooner got the words out than the

trigger of the gun was drawn back and released with a deafening bang.

Thad Hanson reined in his blue roan gelding and stopped to listen. Had that been gunfire he'd heard? He continued to sit as still as a statue, listening for any indication that he had actually heard a shot fired. The second loud pop of a handgun confirmed his suspicion and sent a sickening dread coursing throughout his body. Was the game warden in trouble? Had she had a run-in with old Morty and needed to defend herself? Or had a poacher invaded their private sanctuary in search of a trophy animal? Either way, someone was firing shots on a designated wilderness area, as well as private property. It was illegal and he was going to find out what they were up to and why they felt the need to disturb the peace and quiet.

Urging Blue into a gallop, he rounded the eastern side of Whisper Lake and headed toward the area where the shots had come from. He knew the game warden intended to take water samples to assess the quality of the lake. He'd warned her about Morty and she'd assured him that she would be on the lookout. Unfortunately, a bull moose could be cantankerous at the best of times, but meeting up with one at the beginning of the rut was like running into a full-on disaster just looking for a place to happen. With an over six feet spread across his massive antlers and standing almost seven feet tall at the shoulders, Morty was all muscle with a real bad attitude. Whisper Lake was his well-established territory and the animal would tangle with a military tank in order to maintain his superior status with the herd of cows he'd attracted. The trouble was, Thad wasn't entirely certain the tank would win in a skirmish with the ornery moose. What chance would Game Warden Caldwell have if she'd met up with old Morty? Just the thought caused his stomach to twist into a tight knot and he urged Blue into a full-on run.

As he and the gelding approached the south end of the lake, Thad spotted a red-and-white quadcopter drone hovering over something in the knee-high grass. His heart stopped when the machine fired another shot. He couldn't quite tell what it was aimed at, but he caught a glimpse of something red on the ground as it rolled to the right. Pulling back on the reins,

Thad drew his rifle from the leather scabbard attached to his saddle to use the scope in order to get a closer look. He immediately recognized the red shirt of a Wyoming game warden lying on the ground in a fetal position as the drone took another shot at her. She jerked to the other side and just when he thought the drone would fire again, it suddenly changed direction. As if it had become aware of his presence, it started flying toward him. Thad barely got a look at the buzzing menace and the pistol mounted below a camera on the undercarriage before it fired off a shot that whizzed past his left ear, causing an annoying ringing. Without giving his actions a second thought, Thad leveled his rifle on it and fired. The drone dropped to the ground like a rock.

Thad gave Blue a nudge with his knees, and the horse took off like a shot to the spot where Game Warden Caldwell lay curled into a tight ball with her hands and arms covering her head. Pulling his horse to a shuddering stop, he jumped from the saddle to kneel beside her.

"Were you shot?" he asked urgently. She remained silent and still, ratcheting his fear up another notch. He reached to place his fingers along the carotid artery in her neck to check for a pulse. It was faster than what was considered normal, but the beat was strong and steady. "Come on, lady. Talk to me."

Just when he thought she might be unconscious, she asked, "Is it…gone?"

Releasing a relieved breath, he pushed his wide-brimmed hat off his forehead and sat back on his heels. "Well, not exactly. But I can guarantee it won't hurt you now. Are you okay?"

Instead of answering, she moved her arms from around her head and, frowning, pushed up to a sitting position. "What do you mean by 'not exactly'?"

He pointed toward the red and white pieces of shattered thermoplastic about fifteen feet from them. "Its remains are over there. It gave me no choice but to shoot first and ask questions later."

"I haven't seen anyone else the entire time I've been here. Was that yours? Were you the one playing cat and mouse with me?" she demanded, looking at him with no small amount of suspicion in her sky blue eyes. "What was the point of shooting at me and purposely missing?"

Her accusing expression didn't exactly blindside him. He could understand how it would seem suspicious, since she had never met him before and he was the only other person around. And he wasn't all that offended by her anger, either. She'd been on the receiving end of someone's cruel game and no doubt afraid for her life. Anger wasn't an uncommon reaction to that kind of fear.

He shook his head in disgust. "No, that drone was definitely not mine. My family makes every effort to keep Cougar Mountain a true wilderness area. ATVs, drones and anything like them are strictly prohibited."

"You're a member of the Hanson family?" she asked, looking surprised.

Nodding, he stood up and stuck out his hand, giving her an apologetic smile. "I'm sorry. I should have identified myself first thing. I'm Thad Hanson."

"It's nice to meet you, Dr. Hanson," she said, as she accepted his hand and allowed him to help her to her feet.

When she gasped and shifted her weight to one foot, he asked, "Are you all right?"

"I lost my footing and tweaked my ankle," she said. "It's nothing. Really."

"If you're sure…"

"I am. I'm sure I'll be able to walk it off, but thank you for your concern." She smiled and his heart stalled for a couple of beats. Game Warden Caldwell was pretty. Very pretty. "And thank you for your help. I'm Carrie Caldwell."

"It's nice to meet you, too. Please, call me Thad." When he felt the slight tug of her hand he reminded himself to let go of it. Disgusted with himself for making things awkward, as usual, he cleared his throat. "Since you, uh, didn't have time to tour our operation today, I thought I'd ride over here to introduce myself and see if you needed help."

"I'm very glad you showed up. You saved my life." She shook her head as she glanced over at the drone wreckage. "If you hadn't come along when you did, I might be nothing more than a fond memory." She started to pick up her tablet and its cover at the same time he bent to reach for them. Their heads met with an uncomfortable thunk, causing her WGFD ball cap to fall off. "Ow!"

"I'm really sorry. Are you all right?" he muttered, picking up the tablet and sleeve, as well as her hat, and handing them to her. Feeling every bit the big, clumsy ox he always turned into whenever he was around a woman—especially a pretty one—he shoved his hands into the hip pockets of his jeans to keep from doing something else that would confirm his status as the country bumpkin of Cougar Mountain.

"Don't worry about it. I'm fine," she insisted, but he winced when he noticed her rubbing at a red spot on her forehead before threading her long blond ponytail through the adjustable back of the cap. "Is this area of the Cougar Mountain Ranch accessible by road?"

"Nope." Back on a more comfortable subject, talking about the ranch and mountain he called home, he shook his head. "The only roads on the ranch are private and used for ranch work or getting from our places to one of the others. We each have our own driveway to get to the main road, but even calling them lanes would be a stretch. And before you ask, we don't use four-wheelers, snowmobiles or trail bikes even on our personal areas of the ranch. We've done our best to keep this mountain and the land around it a true natural habitat for all the wildlife on it."

Entering something on her tablet, she smiled. "I wish more people were as dedicated to the preservation of wildlife and natural habitat as you and your family."

"It started with my great-great…grand…" His voice trailed off when a flash of light glinted off of something along the line of trees behind her.

When she turned to look at him, she frowned. "What's wrong?" She looked over her shoulder. "I don't see anything. What are you staring at?"

"Get down!" Rushing forward, Thad heard the crack of a rifle at the same time he caught Carrie around the waist. Cradling her protectively to his chest to absorb the impact, he pulled them to the ground. The high-pitched whine of the round flew over them, lending an undeniable urgency to their situation. He needed to get himself and Carrie out of the clearing to a cluster of boulders at the edge of the lake. It was the closest available cover. But she wasn't helping matters. On the contrary, she was fighting him like a trapped badger.

"Carrie, we have to get out of here. When I roll to your side, get up and head straight for the boulders at the lake's edge. I'll follow and cover your back."

"Get off of me!" The way she was thrashing around and frantically beating his chest, he didn't think she'd heard a word he had said. He wasn't even sure she was aware of the gunshots. She was struggling like her life depended on getting as far away from him as fast as she could.

When another shot rang out and the slug whizzed past a little closer than the last one, Thad yelled at her. "Carrie, stop fighting me! Get up, stay in a crouch and run for the boulders! Now!"

TWO

The sound of Thad's raised voice and urgent orders snapped Carrie out of her flashback and had her scrambling to her feet. The loud whine of another round explained why Thad had tackled her and why he was so insistent that she run for the boulders. Someone was trying to kill them!

Ducking as low as she could manage, she ran in a zigzag pattern to the outcropping of rocks on the lakeshore. Just as she ducked behind the massive cluster of boulders, there was a whining ping, followed by a tiny explosion of chipped rocks showering down on her head. She shuddered at the realization of how close the shot had been .

When he army crawled his way to hide behind the boulders with her, Thad asked, "Are you all right? Were you hit?"

"N-no." Her cheeks felt as if they were on fire and she couldn't meet his questioning gaze. When she'd lost control and her PTSD had taken over, she'd reacted as if he'd been assaulting her. She was embarrassed by her actions now that she knew he'd been trying to save her life. She hadn't been plagued by an episode in the last couple of years. While she knew panic attacks could be triggered at any time by almost anything, she'd thought she had everything under control. It bothered her that she obviously didn't. But it bothered her more that Thad Hanson had been witness to her mini meltdown.

She looked at him from beneath her lashes. He hadn't asked her about her reaction, but he had to be wondering why she panicked when he was only trying to keep her from being shot.

He wore a dark frown. "No, you're not all right? Or no, you weren't shot?"

She shook her head, but still couldn't look him in the eye. "Sorry. No, I wasn't hit and yes, I am okay thanks to your quick thinking. Thank you."

"I'm just glad I saw the sunlight glinting off the barrel of the rifle." He moved to look around the boulder to the clearing beyond, then hung his head and sighed heavily. "It looks like when we're finally able to get out of here, it's going to be on foot."

Carrie frowned. "Your horse…"

"Blue is trained not to get spooked by gunfire from the saddle. He trusts me and as long as I'm riding him, he knows I'll take care of him. But when he's riderless he'll bolt like any other horse when it's startled. And right now, he's headed for the barn at a dead run, along with my satellite phone and extra rounds for my rifle." She watched him push his wide-brimmed cowboy hat off his forehead and lean back against one of the massive rocks surrounding them. "Unless whoever fired those shots gives up and moves on, we're stuck here behind these boulders until it gets dark."

"I have my sidearm," she stated, wondering if he thought she was afraid to use it. Considering her reaction when he tackled her, that was most likely the case. "We can return fire."

He shook his head and motioned toward the rifle in his hand. "And I've got my Winchester, but our shooter has a lot more cover than we do—and a better weapon for shooting at this range. Unless he decides to storm our position, we'd be better off letting him use his ammo and save ours."

Their assailant chose that moment to fire several rounds, causing another shower of rock fragments to rain down on them. She watched Thad brush the granite shards from the wide brim of his hat before pointing his rifle between the boulders to look at the tree line through his scope. "So you're really not going to return fire?" she asked.

"Nope." He lowered his gun and sat back. "Doesn't look like he's going anywhere. At least, for a while."

"But he's shooting at us," she said. "If we don't fire back, he could decide to take advantage of our lack of response and advance on us."

Hanson shrugged. "If he does, we'll fire off a round or two and send him running back to the cover of the trees."

She frowned. He seemed so nonchalant about being pinned down at the edge of the lake. It was rather irritating. "But…"

He sighed heavily. "Look, Carrie, I have four rounds left in my rifle. If you have a loaded clip on your service belt and a full one in your gun, we still only have thirty-four rounds of ammunition between us," he said calmly. "That has to last us until we can get to my brother and sister-in-law's place, which is about four miles from here." He cleared his throat and pointed in the direction of the trees as he added, "At some point he's going to have to leave the cover of those trees to check out whether we're still here or we've managed to get away. Conserving our ammunition and waiting until we have a better shot before we start firing off rounds just makes good sense."

What he said was logical. They wanted to take the man into custody for questioning and to make him face justice for his threats, not kill him. And without Thad's horse to evacuate him or the satellite phone to call for help, if they shot the man there wasn't any way they could get the immediate medical attention he might need to save his life.

"Okay, but when *are* we going to get out of here?" she asked, hating the feeling of being trapped. She took her cell phone from her vest pocket. "Should I call for backup from the Eagle Fork PD or the state highway patrol?"

He shook his head. "There's no cell service up here. We didn't want a cell tower interfering with our plans to keep it a wilderness area."

Her heart sank when she realized she didn't have any bars. Panic was rising in her throat, and it was getting harder and harder to swallow it down. She needed time and space to herself in order to process what had happened and calm herself after her reaction to his innocent attempt to protect her. Sitting barely three feet from him, unable to walk away, wasn't going to allow that to happen. *Dear Lord, please help me hold it together until I can take the time to figure this out and come to terms with it.*

"If we wait until dark, we've got a good chance of slipping out…of here…unnoticed." He sounded distracted, but before she could ask him what was wrong, he sat up, aimed his rifle and stared through the scope. "We should start keeping track of the rounds we have left," he said as he pulled the trigger. "That's one down and thirty-three to go."

When she heard the sound of someone running away, she realized he'd saved them again. She'd been so obsessed with getting control over herself, she hadn't heard their assailant approaching. Taking a deep breath to clear her head, she came to the conclusion that Thad Hanson was right. She might as well get used to the fact that they weren't going anywhere until after dark and they needed to conserve their ammunition.

He sat back against one of the boulders and rested his rifle across his lap. "Well, now he knows we're still here and not going down without a fight."

"Did you get a good look at the guy? Were you able to recognize him?" she asked anxiously. If he could describe the guy in detail, maybe she could figure out who their assailant was.

He nodded. "I did get a fairly good look at him, but I've never seen him before."

Carrie glanced down at the tablet in her hand. She had all but forgotten she still held it and was actually a bit surprised she hadn't dropped it in their mad scramble to get to the boulders. "If you can describe him, I'll include it in the APB I'll issue for his arrest as soon as we get somewhere with internet service," she said, tapping the device to turn it on. "What were his hair and eye colors? Was he tall or short?"

He frowned in obvious concentration. "Kind of long, dark blond, shaggy looking hair, like he hadn't had a haircut in a long time. I couldn't really tell the color of his eyes, but he didn't look to be as tall as me. I'm six feet three inches and I'd say he's an inch or two under six feet, maybe a little shorter. And he looked pretty skinny, like he could use a month or two of good, hearty meals. He's also fairly young. If his scraggly beard is any indication, he's probably in his late teens or just over twenty."

"What was he wearing?"

"Green camo pants, shirt and ball cap." He stopped for a moment to stare off into space before he finished. "And I'm pretty sure he had on either combat or lace-up work boots."

"So he wasn't wearing Western boots?" she asked to be sure.

"Nope." Thad grinned. "They definitely weren't Tony Lamas or Durangos," he said, pointing to his own scuffed cowboy boots.

Her heart stuttered at how nice looking Dr. Thad Hanson was when he smiled. Dismayed that she'd even given his good looks a second thought, she took a deep breath and concentrated on her tablet. She wasn't interested in him or any other man. Period. "Anything else? Any visible marks like scars or tattoos?"

He shook his head. "I didn't notice any scars, but that doesn't mean they aren't there. And I was too busy trying *not* to shoot him to really pay that much attention to whether or not he had ink. Besides, the way he was dressed hid most of his skin."

Carrie entered all the information into her tablet, then checked her watch as she settled back against one of the boulders sheltering them. They had approximately three hours before it got dark and they could make their attempt to get away from the man trying to kill them. Glancing up, she caught Thad watching her. She knew he wondered why she had reacted to him the way she had. She'd been wondering the same thing, herself. And when she figured it out, she might try to give him a vague, simplified explanation. Until then, she intended to forget about her panicked response and concentrate on staying alive.

Thad groaned when he noticed the dark storm clouds gathering in the southwestern sky. Although cloud cover would make it easier to escape later on by blocking the light of the full moon, from the looks of the thunderheads now, they were also promising a cold, extremely wet four-mile hike to his brother's place. He checked his watch. They had about a half hour before it would be dark enough to make their escape. Hopefully there wouldn't be any lightning to illuminate the landscape as they left the shelter of the boulders to sprint across the clearing.

He glanced over at the blond-haired, blue-eyed game warden making notes on her electronic tablet. She had spent the majority of the two and a half hours they'd been pinned down working on the device and avoiding eye contact with him. He'd tried a couple of times to start a conversation with her about her career as a Wyoming game and fish officer, but it hadn't taken long for an uneasy silence to cause him to give up. Their assailant had tried a couple more times to sneak up on them, but Thad had sent the jerk running back into the timberline with well-placed warning shots. After that, he had spent his time thinking about Carrie's reaction to him when he had pulled her to the ground and how he could have handled the situation differently.

He hadn't meant to scare her, but if he'd hesitated, she might not be alive to send him all those suspicious looks. Sighing heavily, he stared down at his loosely clasped hands between his bent knees. Any way he looked at it, he'd done the best he could. Anything less could have very well resulted in one or both of them being killed.

As he sat there thinking about it, he decided he shouldn't be all that surprised by her response when he'd tackled her. He was a fairly big guy and he'd probably looked like a steamroller coming at her and felt like a bulldozer hitting her when he'd taken her down. *Way to make a lasting impression on the lady, Hanson. And not a good one.*

Focused on his disgust with himself for being more like a bull in a china shop than a knight in shining armor, he startled when he heard a clap of thunder. He whipped his head around to look at the ominous bank of clouds in the western sky. He'd all but forgotten about the storm moving in on them. He needed to get his head back in the game. Their survival just might depend on it.

"That doesn't sound good," Carrie said, looking up from her tablet.

Thad shook his head. "It's still far enough out that there's a chance it will get dark before the rain sets in." He lifted his rifle and scanned the woods and clearing to make sure their assailant wasn't trying to sneak up on them again.

"How much longer until the sun sets?" she asked, turning to look at the ugly, roiling clouds approaching from the west.

He checked his watch. "It shouldn't be more than ten minutes or so." Lowering his rifle, he rested it across his legs. "Those thunderheads are still on the other side of that mountain at the far end of the valley. Once they top it, it's going to be like somebody switched off a light and we should be able to make it to the edge of the bulrushes without drawing a lot of attention."

He withheld telling her there was a chance that the shooter could have a night scope on his rifle or night vision goggles that would enable him to know exactly when they left the shelter of the boulders. But she was smart enough to figure out that possibility on her own.

"I suppose we should be ready to go as soon as the clouds reach the mountaintop," she said, placing her tablet in its protective sleeve.

He nodded. "When we make a break for the taller weeds, I'm going to put myself between you and the trees where Drone Jerk is hiding. Stay on my left side and I'll keep pace with you."

"Why would you do that?" she asked, looking startled by his statement. "I'm law enforcement. I should be the one protecting you."

"It just makes sense. Think about it, Carrie." His gaze locked with hers. "For one thing, I make a bigger target and can block any shots he takes at you. And for another, I wouldn't be much of a man if I thought about myself and didn't do everything I possibly can to protect you."

Carrie narrowed her eyes and shook her head. "Thank you for your consideration, but I'm perfectly capable of taking care of myself. I'm a trained game warden, as well as an officer of the law. I'm supposed to be protecting you. It's my job."

"And I respect that." He shrugged one shoulder. "If it makes you feel better, think of me as your backup. But I want this guy caught and you're the game warden handling the investigation to do that. Once you turn in your report, he's going to be facing some extremely serious jail time for a laundry list of violations, along with the attempted murder of two people. Don't you think he'll want to take you out before you have a chance to file that APB?"

Instead of answering him, she asked, "Do you have any idea who the shooter could be or why he's determined to kill us? Is there someone you don't get along with or argued with recently?"

"I could ask you the same." He frowned. "Why would you automatically assume that I'm the one he's after? I already told you I didn't recognize him as being anyone I know or ever met, for that matter. Besides, he was shooting at you before I arrived and the only time he shot at me was when I rode up and witnessed him trying to kill you."

He found her nibbling on her lower lip as she gave his questions some thought. Absolutely fascinating. He swallowed hard and did his best not to stare. There wasn't anything about her that he didn't find mesmerizing. *Stand down, Hanson. You're not any woman's idea of a white knight or even anyone interesting. You're plain old Thad Hanson, country vet and backwoods bumpkin.*

"I arrested several members of a poaching ring about a year ago when I was stationed up along the Montana border," she said, completely unaware of the effect she had on him. "One of them threatened me." She shook her head. "But he was sentenced to almost twelve years in prison and won't be eligible for parole or early release for several more years."

"Was he the only one to get jail time?"

"Yes, but the others faced fines and other consequences."

He thought about what she'd told him. "Does my description fit any of them?"

"None of them were that young—but I guess this could be the son of one of those men."

"Could be," Thad agreed. "Maybe he's trying to get even with you for busting up their ring, sending his dad or his dad's friend to jail."

"That would be rather stupid, don't you think?" she said, frowning.

"It's been my experience that criminals aren't the brightest bulbs in the chandelier." He gave her a lopsided grin. "They all think they're smart enough to get away with their crimes, but the number of inmates in the prison system tells an entirely different story."

He could see she was considering his words as she slipped her tablet sleeve into the inside pocket of her insulated vest before zipping it closed. "If he's shooting at me because he thinks he has an axe to grind and he's shooting at you because you saw him shooting at me, then it doesn't matter who he shoots at first, we're both in danger now."

Realizing the last traces of daylight were

fading away as the clouds topped the mountain in the distance, he raised his rifle to look through the scope. Satisfied the sniper wasn't advancing on them, he lowered his gun and smiled. "Trust me, that's the very reason why I intend to do everything I possibly can to keep both of us alive."

THREE

Carrie stared at Thad when she heard the ominous thunder rumble from the dark bank of clouds as the storm quickly closed in on the valley. Trust this cowboy veterinarian? She wasn't so sure about that.

It wasn't personal. He seemed like a good person. But she'd learned the hard way not to trust easily and especially when it came to most men. Since she escaped the smothering hold that Chip Wilford had on her seven years ago, the only men she'd placed her complete faith and trust in were her father and two older brothers. And that was the way it was going to stay. She'd go along with Thad Hanson just as long as she agreed that his plan was the safest way to proceed. When that ceased to be the case, she'd rely on her own instincts and choose her own path.

As darkness shrouded the valley, a light rain began to fall, then rapidly turned into an all-out downpour. Her vest and ball cap provided very little protection from the cold, falling water. She wasn't sure whether the chill snaking up her spine was due to the frigid rain or the fear that they would be shot like ducks in a carnival arcade game when they ran for the cover of the reeds and cattails.

"Time to go," Thad said, shifting to kneel beside her. "Do you think your ankle will hold up until we can get across the clearing?"

"I think so," she said, hoping it would. "I've purposely left my hiking boots on and loosened the laces just a bit to accommodate the swelling. The top of the boot being above the ankle will add a fair amount of support." She hadn't tried putting her weight on it since they'd taken shelter behind the boulders, but surely it would last until we covered the short distance. It had to. Their lives could very well depend on it.

"Sounds good," he said, nodding. "When we get to our feet, I want you to crouch down and stay close to my left side. Run as fast you can and don't stop until we reach the bulrushes on the other side of the clearing."

"But what if I can't…"

He shook his head. "Don't worry. I'm not going to run off and leave you. I'll make sure I'm between you and him all the way across the clearing no matter what pace you set. If by chance I get shot and go down, don't stop. Keep going. You got that?" When she opened her mouth to object, he took her by the hand, pulled her up as he got to his feet and stepped out from behind the shelter of the boulders. "Let's go," he urged, denying her the chance to protest as he pulled her along with him.

As they sprinted across the open area, she expected to hear gunfire and possibly feel the excruciating pain of a bullet hitting its mark. But the continuous deafening thunder overhead drowned out any other sound as they quickly raced the distance and plunged into the ten-feet-tall reeds and cattails growing on the other side of the clearing. "I can't believe...we made it...without being shot," she said, trying to catch her breath. She hadn't realized until they reached the shelter of the bulrushes that she'd held her breath, awaiting a bullet to take one or both of them down during their mad dash. And amazingly, her ankle was sore but not to the point she had a lot of trouble walking on it.

Thad nodded. "He fired at us at least once and possibly twice, but he's either a lousy shot or he's letting us know that we might have won this battle, but he's not calling off the war."

Sheltered from the shooter's sight by the tall weeds, she was drenched and shivering from the cold rain, her teeth chattering like a pair of windup choppers from a novelty shop. "Wh-what now? D-do we…st-start out for… your brother's p-place? Will…they be okay… w-with us…b-barging in…on th-them?"

"They aren't even home and wouldn't mind us taking shelter there even if they were," he insisted. "They're on their honeymoon in Hawaii."

Holding his rifle in one hand, he put his arm around her shoulders and pulled her against his side; he was sure in an effort to shelter her from some of the rain. But as much as she appreciated the gentlemanly gesture, it was raining so hard nothing was going to stop them from being drenched. "It's going to take us about an hour and a half to two hours to get there on foot," he said apologetically as he rubbed his big hand up and down her arm, trying to keep her warm. Staying in a crouched position, he steered them through the wall of giant grasses.

To her surprise, instead of the overwhelming anxiety that normally would have followed being this close to a strange man, she found Thad's nearness wasn't at all unpleasant and caused an awareness that made her heart skip a beat. In fact, the most unsettling thing was how she *didn't* feel threatened. A little uneasy, maybe, but nothing like she would have expected. She wasn't sure what to make of that.

"It doesn't make any sense."

"What was that?" he asked, leaning his head closer to hers. "It's raining so hard I didn't catch what you said."

She hadn't realized she'd spoken aloud. "Nothing of any importance," she murmured, wondering what was wrong with her. His firm lips and warm breath feathered over her ear. The reverberation of his rich baritone made her insides hum. *Stop it! You're absolutely not interested in him or any other man. Men are nothing but pain physically, mentally and emotionally.* Trying to refocus on what really mattered here—putting distance between them and Whisper Lake—she said, "I'm wondering if our assailant will try to follow us in this storm. He'd have to be a glutton for punishment in this downpour." No sooner had the words left her mouth than it began to rain like someone pouring water out of a bucket.

"If he's smart, he won't follow us for long," Thad agreed, guiding her to the edge of the bulrushes. Beyond the thick grass, there was a path disappearing into the tall evergreen forest surrounding the base of Cougar Mountain. "The canopy of trees should shelter us from some of the rain. Not a lot, but it'll be better than nothing."

"At this point, I don't think it will matter," she said as rivulets of cold rainwater ran down her face to drip off her chin. Looking up at him, she watched water channeled by the wide brim of his cowboy hat drain off the back almost like a mini waterfall. "There isn't a dry spot on me and I doubt you're much better off."

His deep chuckle as he shook his head caused a warmth to spread throughout her chest. "I couldn't be any more soaked if I'd jumped in the lake." When lightning flashed, followed by a deafening clap of thunder, he motioned for her to precede him down the path. "We just have to follow this trail for a couple of hours and it will come out behind my brother's barn."

"Why don't you take the lead?" she asked as he urged her down the well-worn path. "You know more about where we're headed than I do."

"Because the jerk back there in that grove of lodgepole pines will eventually figure out which way we went, and I intend to be between you and him on the outside chance he catches up."

Thad was never so glad to see his brother's barn come into view. He exhaled a sigh of pure relief as they let themselves through the feedlot gates to cross Sean's backyard. He and Carrie were completely soaked and, with the evening temperature dropping into the lower forties, chilled to the point they were close to becoming hypothermic. Stopping at the edge of the porch, he reached down by the bottom step to retrieve the key hidden under the small wooden keg that his new sister-in-law had turned into a planter. If he hadn't been so miserably wet and cold, he might have laughed. Since his FBI agent brother, Sean, had fallen in love with the woman he'd kept safe after a disastrous bank robbery, his now wife, Bailey, and their mother had decided the ranch house needed a feminine touch. When they got married a few months ago, their mom and Bailey started changing something whenever his mom and dad came for a visit from their retirement home in Arizona. Fortunately, Sean didn't seem to mind. His brother was so deeply in love, if Bailey wanted to paint the house hot pink and decorate the great room with hearts, cupids and fuzzy kittens, Sean would be fine with it as long as it made her happy.

When Thad placed his hand on Carrie's lower back to guide her up the steps to the back door, he could tell by her shivering and stiff movements that she was chilled to the bone. "I'll build a fire in the fireplace and find something for you to change into, if you'd like to take a hot shower to warm up. You can also wash and dry your clothes," he offered, letting them into the mud room. The dry warmth of the log home immediately surrounded them like a thick blanket. It was a welcome relief from the cold, driving rain. He pointed to her boots as he kicked off his. "While you're in the shower, I'll clean the mud off our boots and put them by the fireplace to dry out."

"Are you sure your brother and sister-in-law will be okay with us making ourselves at home?" she asked, untying her hiking boots to slip them and her soggy socks off. He noticed that her feet were thankfully a healthy pink, instead of the bluish gray he'd feared they might be.

He nodded as he turned to lock the door. "In case of an emergency, we all know where the hidden keys are located at each others' houses. Trust me, this is exactly what they'd want us to do. They'd be proud to offer us somewhere to stay that was safe. Family comes first for us, always."

"How many Hanson siblings are there?" she asked as she followed him down the hall toward the guest bedroom.

"There are four of us—all brothers."

"Oh, wow!" She laughed. "If you and your brothers are anything like my two brothers, your mother must have the patience of Job."

He chuckled. "I'm sure she'd be the first to admit we were a pretty big handful. And I've heard her say more than once that she had to contend with five boys—my dad being the oldest." Carrie laughed as he showed her to the guest bedroom and opened the door. "The bathroom is private and has a lock on the door. There should be shower gel and shampoo in the cabinet, along with towels and a bathrobe." When she gave him a questioning glance, he smiled. "Our mom taught us to be ready for guests whether they're expected or not."

"Your mother sounds like a very wise woman," she said, walking into the guest room.

"She's pretty on top of things," he agreed as he backed from the room. "I'll, um, go see what I can find for you to wear while our clothes are being washed and dried. Once I pull a few things together, I'll leave them on the bench at the end of the bed."

Closing the door behind him, he shook his head as he went on a clothes search. Now that the immediate danger was behind them, it was harder to put aside thoughts about how he was alone with a beautiful woman. Yes, Carrie was stunning—and also sweet and strong and capable—but there was no chance she'd ever be interested in him.

From the time he was old enough to notice that girls were nicer to watch than a ball game, he'd felt like a fish out of water around them. They'd fascinated, frustrated and confused him to the point he had been relieved when he finally found a girl in college that seemed to want to be with him. They dated for years, until he was convinced she was the one and asked her to marry him.

But just like he always did with women, he'd misunderstood the situation. He'd proposed the night he graduated with his doctorate in veterinary medicine—and she'd turned him down flat, bluntly telling him that she had no desire to marry a rancher who lived in the middle of nowhere. She'd then added that when she had children she didn't want them to be country bumpkins like he was, nor did she want to marry a man who was around dirty, smelly animals all the time. Suffering from a broken heart and a thoroughly bruised ego, he'd decided that he would be better off devoting himself to the care and well-being of animals and forget about being in a romantic relationship. He had always been much better with dogs, cats, horses or even a bear with a sore paw than he had with any woman, and her rejection just drove that lesson home.

When he found a couple of sweatshirts and sweatpants in a box labeled Donation in the bottom of Sean's closet, he plucked them out and snagged a couple of pairs of thick tube socks from a dresser drawer on his way out of the room. He made a quick stop to deposit one of the shirts, pants and a pair of socks on the bench at the end of the bed in the guest bedroom, and then hurriedly headed for the other guest room across the hall. Hopefully he'd be able to shower, get dressed and have something ready for them to eat by the time she made it back to the kitchen.

Fifteen minutes later, Thad had just finished placing their cleaned boots on the hearth in the great room, tossed his sodden clothes into the washer in the laundry room and entered the kitchen to crack some eggs in a bowl, when Carrie walked in carrying her wet clothing. He swallowed hard and diverted his gaze to the bowl of eggs. She'd blow-dried her long blond hair and the silky waves hung down past her shoulders, making her look softer and more approachable. But it was the clothes he'd found for her to wear that made her look absolutely adorable. The sweatshirt hung all the way to her knees. It was fortunate the too-long sweatpants had elastic around the bottom of the legs or they would have constantly tripped her as she walked.

He shook his head and concentrated on the eggs to keep from saying something stupid. "The laundry room is through that door," he said, pointing to the far side of the large kitchen. "I've already dumped my clothes in the washer."

"I'll go ahead and start the wash cycle, then after we eat, the clothes should be ready to go into the dryer," she offered, hitching at the waist of the pants to pull them higher.

"That sounds like a plan." He reached into the refrigerator to grab a bag of shredded cheese. "How do you like your eggs?"

"Sunny side up."

"I should probably clarify my question," he said, grinning. "What do you want *in* our scrambled eggs? Cheese? Onions?" He turned to glance back into the refrigerator, then looked in the freezer, spotting a few more containers. "Maybe some chopped ham, bacon, red and green bell peppers?"

"Let me guess. You don't know much about cooking, do you?" she asked, walking into the laundry room.

"I know enough not to starve, but I discovered early in my college days that I can make some really creative sandwiches that don't require anything more than a minute or two in the microwave," he answered when she returned.

Her smile caused a warm, fuzzy feeling

to spread throughout his chest. "Sounds like you have the ingredients for a yummy omelet. Would you like for me to make a couple of them for us?"

He blew out a relieved breath. "I'd like that a lot." Cooking for himself was one thing, it was either something he could eat or if it was suitable, feed to his dog, Max. But making something that someone else found edible was an entirely different matter. "Besides making a pot of coffee, what can I do to help?"

"Since the ham, onions and peppers are already chopped and the cheese is shredded, you can find some plates for me to dish up the omelets and then set the table."

Thad got busy starting the coffee maker, set the requested plates on the counter next to the stove, and by the time he finished putting out silverware, the coffee was ready and so were the omelets. He stood behind her chair to hold it for her. Once she was seated, he slid into the chair next to hers, then held out his hand. When she placed her hand in his, he bowed his head. "Lord, please bless this food we are about to eat and keep us safe in Your care from those who seek to harm us. Amen."

"Amen." She paused for a moment before

she raised her head to look at him. "Thank you. I wasn't aware..."

"That I'm a believer?" He smiled as he sliced into the delicious-smelling food with the side of his fork. "Other than deciding I was too cool to go to church for a short time when I was a teenager, and then losing my way for a while when I started dating the wrong girl in college, I've always believed."

She remained quiet for a moment, as if coming to a decision. "I, um, had a similar experience when I was in college, but thankfully it didn't take me long to find my way back to my faith."

"I think a lot of kids go through something similar before they straighten themselves out," he said, taking a bite of the omelet. He closed his eyes to savor the delicious meal. "This is awesome. Thank you for saving us from some less than perfect scrambled eggs."

"You're welcome," she said, smiling as she took a bite.

They made comfortable small talk while they ate. When they were done, Thad scooted his chair back from the table and rose to take their plates to the sink for rinsing and loading into the dishwasher. "Why don't you refill our coffee cups and settle down by the fireplace while I put our clothes in the dryer?"

"What time is it?" she asked, pouring herself and him another cup of the strong brew. He normally didn't drink coffee at night, but being so tired from the afternoon and evening threats, he was almost positive it wouldn't keep him awake.

"Almost ten thirty," he called from the laundry room. He picked up his cell phone and checked to see if it had escaped without becoming waterlogged. When it went through the reboot function, he nodded in satisfaction. "If you want to go on into the great room and settle down on the couch in front of the fire, I'll join you in a few minutes. I need to call one of my other brothers to let him know what's going on and ask him to come over in the morning to take us back to my place."

"Sounds good. I'm happy to get settled in front of the fireplace," she said, once again hitching at the too-long sweatpants. "That hot shower and these dry clothes have helped a lot, but I'm still a bit chilled. Besides, if I can get my tablet to work I'm going to send my report to the regional office and have an APB issued for our assailant."

Giving her the house's Wi-Fi password, he

watched her turn and pad across the hardwood floor in socked feet as he dialed his brother Blane. It rang several times before his brother answered, causing Thad to grimace. Blane was going to be none too happy about being awakened in what his early-to-bed-early-to-rise brother considered to be the middle of the night.

"You'd better have a real good reason for waking me up, Dolittle," Blane groused, using the nickname he'd hung on Thad when he graduated from veterinarian school. "I have to be up at four in the morning to feed a bunch of hungry cows and they don't like it when I'm grouchy."

"Sorry, bro," Thad apologized. "I would have called Levi, but he's on duty at the Eagle Fork fire station tonight and I needed to let you know what's going on." Explaining what had taken place at Whisper Lake and how they had escaped to Sean's part of the ranch, he asked, "Could you come over tomorrow after you get the cattle fed and take us back to my place?"

Blane's voice was suddenly all business. "Are you sure you and the lady game warden are all right? I can drive over now if you need me to."

"Thanks, but we're fine for the time being," Thad assured him. "With the storm, the guy would have to be a pretty great tracker to figure out which direction we went."

"Well, let me know if you change your mind," Blane said. "Since it quit raining, I can be there in ten minutes if I saddle Captain and cut across the pastures." He paused for a moment before he spoke again. "Did you see Morty while you were up at Whisper Lake? You know how touchy he gets this time of year."

"No, I assume he's found a few moose cows to spend time with for the next several weeks."

"I don't know why, but I really like that moose."

Thad couldn't help but laugh. "That moose tried to stomp you into the ground at least twice that I know of and the last time, you swore you were going to catch him and sell him to a zoo if he tried to do it again."

His brother's voice took on a haughty tone. "You wouldn't understand. Ours is a complicated relationship."

"If you say so, bro."

Thad took a deep breath. "Yeah. Listen, just in case this jerk we ran into today at

Whisper Lake actually does show up to try turning us into ducks in a shooting gallery, keep your phone handy."

"Will do." Blane added, "And tomorrow when I get over to Sean's, if you're not there, I'll assume you had to bug out like we had to do a few times in Afghanistan. If that happens, where do you want me to meet you and the lady game warden for evac?"

"The ruins of the old lodge," Thad answered, without hesitation.

"That thing burned even before Dad was a twinkle in Grandpa's eye," Blane stated flatly. "Are you sure that's where you want to meet up?"

"Yup. Remember that log toolshed? The fire didn't touch it—and it's well hidden by all the trees that have grown up around it."

"I know where you're talking about."

"It's almost due north of your place and if you want to come on horseback and bring a couple of saddled mounts with you, it would be faster than trying to get to that upland valley by taking the old logging road. I'll call and let you know if we're on the run. Otherwise, I'll see you here at Sean's place in the morning," Thad finished.

"Actually, that's a pretty good plan, little brother," Blane finally said, yawning.

"I'm glad you approve," Thad answered dryly. "Now, go back to sleep. You need to be your charming self when you feed those cows tomorrow morning."

"Will do. You and the lady game warden take care," Blane said with a hint of mischief in his voice.

"We will. And just for the record, her name is Carrie," Thad shot back, immediately sorry he'd corrected his brother. "Er, Game Warden Caldwell," he added hastily.

"Oh, so you're on a first name basis with the lady, are you?" His brother's teasing tone caused Thad to grind his teeth.

"Goodnight, Blane. I'll see you in the morning," he said, disconnecting the call before his brother could goad him into saying something else he would end up regretting.

After making his way around the house to check every window and door to make sure they were locked securely, he took their clothing from the dryer, folded them and took them into the great room. He found Carrie, wrapped in one of his sister-in-law's colorful crocheted afghans, sound asleep on the big leather couch in front of the fireplace. Setting the stack of clothes on the coffee table beside their firearms and the extra ammunition he'd borrowed from his brother's gun safe, he sank into the matching armchair and stretched out his legs in front of him. Now that he'd warmed up, he was bone tired and barely able to keep his eyes open. He'd just rest a few minutes, then wake Carrie and send her down the hall to the guest room, while he bedded down on the couch in case Drone Jerk was successful at tracking them and tried to break in.

The next thing Thad knew, the sound of shattering glass had him instantly awake and on his feet. The fire had burned down to glowing red embers, and a quick check of the antique clock on the mantel indicated that he and Carrie had been asleep for a couple of hours.

"What was that?" she asked, shoving her hair away from her face as she rose to a sitting position on the couch.

"Somebody is trying to break in," he said, turning out the lights and grabbing their boots from the hearth. He handed Carrie hers and pulled on his. Reaching for their guns, he grabbed his jacket and her insulated vest. "Come on," he said, ushering her down the dark hall. "We need to get out of here."

FOUR

"If someone is breaking into the back of the house, why aren't we going out the front?" Carrie asked, pulling on her vest as Thad closed and locked the guest room door behind them.

He shook his head as he shrugged into his jacket, then went to the window across the room to push the curtains aside. "If I had to guess, I'd say that since he hasn't entered through the kitchen window he broke, he's headed around to the front to intercept us as we leave." Releasing the lock on the guest room window, he pushed up the sash. "That's why we're going out this way. It's a quick sprint from this end of the house to a trail leading to the backup rendezvous location where my brother and I planned to meet." He threw one of his long legs over the sill followed by the other and jumped down to the ground. "Climb out and I'll help you down."

"I can jump," she said, sitting on the sill. She swung her legs over the side and got ready to jump. She appreciated the way he tried to look out for her, but, she still couldn't bring herself to trust him completely. He was a man and she'd learned the hard way that some men had a dark side they kept hidden until...

"Don't jump," he cautioned, distracting her from her disturbing thoughts. Before she could refuse his command, he quickly propped his rifle against the side of the house, reached up and caught hold of her behind the knees to pull her to him. "You were limping on the hike from Whisper Lake, and I'd rather not make your injured ankle worse from jumping six feet down onto uneven ground." Conceding the point, she let him help her down. Once she was standing beside him, he picked up his rifle, caught her hand in his and, pulling her along, crossed the distance to the trees as he finished his explanation. "If your ankle really starts bothering you and you find you can't run, let me know and I'll carry you until we're farther up the trail.

We need to move fast. I don't want him knowing exactly which direction we're heading."

As she followed him into the thick forest, she wondered where this rendezvous point was. Although it had stopped raining and their clothing was dry, if they went too far up the mountain, the temperature would be much colder and they might even encounter snow. She was used to being out in colder conditions and she was certain that he was, too, but her insulated vest and his flannel-lined denim jacket, although perfect for the chilly temperatures of mid-fall around the base of the mountain, wouldn't be enough for the extremes they might encounter at the higher elevations.

They ran along the narrow trail for some time before it split, with one path going farther up the mountain, while the other seemed to move off through the thick forest on a more horizontal route. Thad veered onto the one going through the thick forest and immediately stepped off the trail to trot through the trees.

"Where are you going?" she asked. It was so dark she could barely see and it amazed her that they hadn't jogged into a tree or a boulder or even off of a cliff. "Why aren't we staying on the trail?"

"Because with the recent rain we'll leave boot tracks that a blind man could follow," he said in a low whisper. "If we stick to the pine needle carpet just off the trail, we have a good chance of giving whoever this is the slip."

"Good plan," she admitted. What he said made sense and if she'd had more sleep, as well as more warning that they were going to be fleeing for their lives again, she might have thought of it herself. "Do you think…it will work?" She had always considered herself in fairly good shape, but they had been jogging uphill for most of the distance and she was beginning to get winded, not to mention her ankle had started throbbing in time with her elevated heartbeat.

Thad shrugged. "Time will tell, but it's worth a shot, either way." He helped her over a fallen tree, then motioned for her to sit down. "I think it's safe for us to stop here to rest for a few minutes. How's your ankle holding up?"

"It hurts," she reluctantly admitted. "But the top of my hiking boot is helping to support it." He remained standing when she sank down onto the prone tree trunk to catch her breath and check her leg for swelling. She would have wrapped it with an elastic bandage, but she'd fallen asleep before asking about one. Then they'd had to leave in such a hurry, there hadn't been enough time to give it a second thought. "You don't think…he's following us?"

"I haven't heard any sounds indicating a tail since we reached the fork in the trail thirty minutes ago. Up until then, he was making enough noise to wake a dead man." He paused for a moment as if listening, then continued. "For what it's worth, I don't think whoever this is would have been a member of that poaching ring you busted up by the Montana line."

"Why do you say that?"

"Hunters learn how to slip through the woods without making a lot of noise. It becomes second nature for them. Most poachers start out as avid hunters." He shook his head in obvious disgust. "If this guy was more experienced, he'd know how to track us without making so much noise."

"You have a point, but who else could it be? I can't ignore the threats the leader made against my life," she said. "If we stick with the theory that this could be the guy's son, then maybe his dad just never took him on hunting trips so he didn't get the practice. But speaking of family connections, what did you discuss with your brother?" she asked.

He nodded. "You were asleep and I didn't want to wake you. He was going to pick us up tomorrow morning, but I told him our plans were subject to change if the jerk who tried to shoot us showed up at Sean's. We decided if that happened, I'd call and let him know we'd meet him around daylight at a log tool-shed behind an old burned-out lodge at the end of the logging road."

"Do you have cell service on this part of the ranch?" she asked, hoping with all her heart that they hadn't gone beyond signal availability.

He smiled. "That's another reason we stopped here. We're getting close to losing service and I need to give Blane the heads-up that we're meeting at the old lodge, instead of waiting for him at Sean's place."

Carrie frowned as she watched Thad call his brother. She wasn't used to having a man make plans for her personal safety or relying on him to see those plans through. That required believing in someone and being confident they had her best interest at heart. It had been seven years since she'd stopped handing that kind of trust over to anyone outside of her family. Some lessons were learned the hard way and she had the scars, both physical and emotional, to prove that she'd learned hers well. She'd trusted the wrong man and only by the grace of God had she escaped with her life. She wouldn't let herself be put in that position again.

Unfortunately, she didn't have any other choice but to go along with the arrangements Thad and his brother had made. She'd left her cell phone at Thad's brother's house along with her tablet and clothes, so she couldn't even call for police intervention. She sighed heavily. She also didn't have any experience with the trails and paths on Cougar Mountain, and she was going to have to rely on Thad to guide her out of there—once again counting on him for something she'd normally prefer to do for herself.

She glanced down at the oversize gray sweats she'd put on after her shower. While she appreciated him arranging for her to have something to eat and something clean and dry to wear, it would have been a lot easier if she hadn't had to run through the forest with one hand holding up the baggy sweatpants. The only thing besides her vest and boots she'd managed to bring with them was her gun and spare clip of ammunition. After Thad handed them to her as they were making a hasty exit, she'd tucked them into the pocket of her vest and zipped it closed before they fled. But since it was so dark, the weapon really wouldn't do her any good at holding someone off. Due to the lingering heavy cloud cover blocking the moon and stars, she could barely see her hand in front of her face, let alone make out what she was aiming at if she needed to help protect them.

When Thad ended his call and pocketed his cell phone, he sat beside her and, leaning forward, propped his forearms on his bent knees. "Blane will bring a couple of horses for us just before dawn." He paused for a moment before asking, "You do ride, don't you?"

"Does a duck paddle around in a pond?" she shot back, grinning. "I was born and raised on my parents' cattle ranch up by Sheridan. I started riding a horse almost before I could walk."

His deep chuckle caused her heart to skip a beat. "Me, too. But I had to ask. Not everyone in Wyoming is a cowboy or cowgirl. Taking it on faith that someone can ride a horse just because they live in this state is an assumption only an idiot makes."

She nodded. "How far are we from this lodge?"

"A couple of miles," he answered, standing up to stretch. "Do you think your ankle will hold up until we get there?"

"It should be fine. I'm pretty sure it's just a soft tissue injury and not a tendon or ligament issue," she assured him.

"Do you think it could be fractured?" he asked, gazing down at her foot. "I can carry you if you need me to."

"No, that won't be necessary." She shook her head. "I've had a couple of broken bones before and this isn't even close to that level of pain. And if it was broken, I seriously doubt I would have been able to get down the hallway in your brother's house, let alone take off running up a mountain."

He gave her a short nod, then took a deep breath as he leaned close and lowered his voice to just above a whisper. "I had to make sure. Now, to get back to your question. Normally, it would only take us less than an hour to get there, but on a night like this, with heavy cloud cover and your ankle injury, it will probably take twice as long." With his head so close to hers, she could just make out his wide grin. "But I'd rather go a little slower and not end up risking a couple of broken necks by walking off a cliff or taking a tumble down into a ravine."

When she got to her feet, she put a little space between them. "No, neither scenario is appealing." Taking a page from his book, she stretched to keep her muscles from cramping after all of the running they'd done. "I'm ready to move along whenever you are." The words had no sooner left her mouth when the sound of a high-powered rifle split the night air, and bark and pine needles rained down on them.

"Run!" Thad shouted as he grabbed her hand and took off sprinting through the trees.

With his strong hand engulfing hers, Carrie had no choice but to follow and pray they would be able to escape this madness yet again.

Thad took off down the trail, doing his best not to go too fast for Carrie. He didn't want to end up making her fall, possibly injuring her ankle further, but they needed to put as much distance as they could between them and the shooter. Chastising himself for spending too much time at their rest stop, he released her hand and slowed down enough for her to pass him. "Get in front of me."

"Why?" she asked, even as she jogged around him to take the lead.

"Because if he takes another shot, I want to make sure he misses you," he answered truthfully. If someone was going to be shot, he'd gladly take the bullet to keep her safe. She didn't deserve to be hurt or killed because of his negligence.

"How close is he?" she asked as they continued along the trail.

"Save your breath for running and stay on this path," he said, glancing over his shoulder. "We'll talk when I'm sure it's safe to stop."

She nodded and continued putting one foot in front of the other, while he kept watching their six. They hadn't been shot at for the past twenty minutes and Thad was fairly certain the guy hadn't been able to close the distance between them. But he wasn't taking it on faith that the man was giving up the chase. He probably had thermal imaging binoculars or a rifle scope he could use to spot their location. But they weren't too far from the logging road that would lead them to the burned-out lodge, and once they were there, they should be safer. There were places to take shelter there that night vision or thermal imaging devices wouldn't be able to penetrate.

When he recognized a few of the last natural markers signaling they were close to the end of the trail, he tapped her on the shoulder. "There's a bend in the path about…fifty yards up ahead. Once we round that…there will be an outcropping of boulders…to your left. That's where we'll…stop to catch our breath and…rest."

"Good. My leg muscles feel…like they're… on fire."

She sounded out of breath and he couldn't say he was much better off. He felt guilty that they'd had to push so hard to get away. They'd been running for the better part of forty minutes since being shot at. Although it had mostly been at a jog, they were both wearing heavy boots and the grade of the trail had gradually increased as they went along.

"I think we can slow down…and walk the rest of the way," he said, reducing his speed. Careful to keep his voice low, he added, "It wouldn't be a bad idea if we cooled down… before we stop, anyway."

"Do you think…it's safe?" she asked, matching his slower pace.

It wasn't lost on him that her limp was more pronounced than it had been before, and his guilt increased tenfold. "I can't be for sure…but we haven't had to dodge any gunfire…since we took off running."

He slid his arm around her waist to support her when they rounded the bend in the path and walked toward the boulders. To his surprise, she didn't protest and actually leaned on him as they approached the cluster of large granite rocks. In the several hours since they met, he'd got the impression that she didn't like relying on anyone for anything. He wanted to believe that her acceptance of his assistance now meant that she was coming to trust him—but realistically, it probably was testament to the fact that the pain in her ankle had increased significantly, and she didn't have a lot of choice but to accept his help.

He took a deep breath and forced himself to relax when they reached the boulders. She sank down onto one of the shorter ones with a relieved sigh. "We'll rest here for a couple of minutes," Thad said. "This guy couldn't possibly know this mountain as well as I do and

I think he's most likely using a rifle with a night vision or possibly thermal image scope to track us instead of relying on signs along the trail."

"I was thinking the same thing." She didn't sound as out of breath, lessening some of his guilt. "It's too dark to see without it and I doubt he was just firing randomly."

Thad shook his head. "That slug came too close for him to be taking pot shots in the dark. But once we reach the lodge, thermal imaging and night vision won't do him any good."

"Who's doing this and why?" she asked, sounding frustrated. "And why is he so determined to kill us?" There was a distinct edge to her voice, and he hated that she felt so threatened.

"Your guess is as good as mine." When he saw her shiver he didn't know if it was caused by her nerves or if she was chilled. It didn't matter. There wasn't a lot he could do to improve their current situation, but he could lend her his strength, as well as his body heat. Before he could give it much thought, he propped his rifle against one of the boulders, sat beside her and put his arm around her shoulders, pulling her close to his side. He was encouraged by the fact that, although he detected a slight tensing of her muscles, she didn't demand that he let her go. Running his hand up and down her arm, he tried to put her at ease. "You'll warm up again when we start moving."

She nodded. "I'm not sure I've been completely warm since this started. But you'd think I'd be overheated with as much running as we've been doing." They sat in silence for a few minutes before she spoke again. "If he does have a thermal scope, he can't see us here among these boulders, right?" she asked, her voice almost a whisper.

"Right. It's not like what you see in the movies," he answered, just as quietly. "Thermal imaging cameras and scopes can't 'see' through everything. Even most house walls are too dense for anyone to get a definitive heat signature indicating what's inside."

They fell silent and Thad marveled at how at ease he felt with Carrie. It didn't make a lot of sense considering they'd only known each other a few hours. But from what he could tell about her so far, she was straightforward and definitely didn't play games the way some women did. That helped him feel at ease around her—far more so than he ever felt with women who said one thing while they meant another. He never seemed to get things right, misreading signals and situations. It was the main reason he'd given up on relationships right after his failed marriage proposal to his college girlfriend. He stood a better chance at understanding the moods of an ornery bull moose than he did a woman.

"How much farther until we get to the old lodge?" she asked, pulling away from him.

Respecting her need for space, he stood and looked up the logging road. "Not far. Maybe a half mile or so." When he turned back, he noticed her grimace as she gingerly moved her ankle. "We'll go a little slower. It shouldn't take us more than twenty minutes or so. Once we get there, you should be able to stay off your feet and rest for a couple of hours before Blane shows up."

"I can't argue with that," she said, standing up. "I thought I was in shape, but all this running has clearly proven I'm not as fit as I thought I was."

He chuckled. "Shoot yourself a break. You were running uphill most of the time on a bad ankle and aren't wearing the proper shoes for…" His voice trailed off at the sound of a branch breaking and a muttered oath. Grabbing his rifle, he looked up the road, then back at her. "Let's get out of here."

Her eyes widened. "That was the shooter, wasn't it?" she whispered as they broke into a jog.

He nodded as he fell into step with her, then, taking her hand in his, broke into an all-out run. "And if we don't kick it up a notch, he's going to round that bend in the path and have a clear shot at both of us."

FIVE

Carrie gritted her teeth against a fresh wave of pain in her ankle and pushed herself harder in order to keep from slowing them down. *You can do this! You* need *to do this. A sprain has to be a lot less painful than a bullet hole in your back. Keep running!*

Thad suddenly threw an arm around her and steered them off the overgrown road into the thick growth of willows lining the side of it. He motioned for her to crouch down, and once they were well hidden, he placed his index finger to his lips, signaling silence.

As they hunkered behind the bushes, she heard the heavy sound of boots pounding against the hard-packed ground as someone jogged past their hiding place. It wasn't until the sound faded away that she released the breath she hadn't even been aware she was holding.

"Come on," Thad whispered close to her ear as he stood up. He held out his hand to help her to her feet. "We need to move farther off the trail and into the trees before he doubles back to start searching for us in these bushes."

"Is there a way to get to the ruins of the lodge from here, other than the old road?" she asked, glancing at the abandoned lane that was little more than an overgrown path.

Thad nodded as he pushed the boughs of a Douglas fir aside and motioned for her to precede him. "This way will be a little longer and not nearly as clear and easy as the road would be, but there aren't any steep drop-offs or ravines between us and the lodge site."

"Is the shed all that's left of the buildings?" she asked quietly as she gingerly limped around a fallen tree.

"I'm not sure if it would be classified as a building, but besides the shed, there's a root cellar," he answered in a hushed tone. "That's where we'll hide out until my brother shows up around dawn, unless I'm absolutely certain this guy has given up looking for us on this part of the mountain."

Her breath froze in her lungs and she had to struggle to take in air. Just the thought of how closed in it must be in the root cellar, how dark and damp in the underground structure, sent goosebumps shimmering over her skin and caused a sickening dread to settle in her chest. She hadn't always been claustrophobic or afraid of the dark, but after Chip tried to choke her to death, he'd locked her in a small storage room in his apartment building's leaky basement in an effort to keep her from running straight to the cops. Fortunately, the lock had been faulty, and when she'd gained enough strength to flee, she had escaped the cold, clammy closet and gone directly to the nearest police station. Ever since then, even the thought of being trapped, particularly in a small space underground, had her on the verge of a panic attack.

When she stumbled, Thad reached out to put his arm around her waist to support her. "I promise we're almost there, Carrie. Just another hundred yards or so. Do you think you can make it or do you want me to carry you?"

She shook her head, but allowed herself to accept the support he offered. "I'll be able to make it."

Her foot hurt and she knew beyond a shadow of doubt that if she stopped to rest, she wouldn't be able to start up again—not so much because of the injury, but because of the bone-deep exhaustion that was beginning to settle in. They had hiked four miles in the pouring rain from the lake to his brother's house, and after only a couple of hours of sleep, they had been forced to run several miles again. Only this time it had been up the side of a mountain. Her body was reaching the end of its strength.

When they came to the edge of a clearing, Thad stopped behind a grouping of willows and stared a couple of minutes at the brush-and weed-covered area. He was apparently making sure their tormentor wasn't still hanging around. Finally steering her toward a grass-and leaf-covered hump in the landscape, he assured her, "It looks like he doubled back to search for detours along the road that we might have taken."

"This is the root cellar, isn't it?" When he nodded, she swallowed hard and shook her head. "I don't think I can go down in there."

"Why not?" he asked, removing his arm from her waist to inspect the opening. "My brother Levi was up here this past summer and had to take shelter inside it during a severe thunderstorm. He said that, considering it's around a hundred years old, it's in fairly good shape."

"Where's the toolshed you mentioned before?" she asked, desperately looking around for anywhere else they could hide. It was supposed to be nearby. "Why can't we stay in there?"

"The toolshed wouldn't protect us as well from thermal imaging. This is the best place to avoid detection."

"I, uh…just don't think it looks all that safe. It's not very secure, is it?" She hated that her voice cracked. But just the thought of going down into that hole sent a chill snaking down her spine and panic tying her stomach into a tight knot. She shook her head. "I-it… would feel…t-too much…like a…t-tomb."

"It's the safest place for us until Blane gets here," he said gently. He stared at her for several seconds before he stepped forward and wrapped his arms around her, pulling her to his wide chest. "It's going to be all right, Carrie. I'll be right beside you. I promise if something comes down those steps, I won't let it touch you. Whether it's got two legs or four, it will have to go through me first."

His rich baritone and the soothing touch of his hand lightly rubbing her back helped to shore up her emotional strength. Maybe she could get through this without having a panic attack. Or worse yet, a PTSD episode. Using the breathing technique her therapist had suggested, she breathed deeply and slowly for several moments before she managed to explain. "I'm not worried about the animals that could wander inside."

"Then what is it holding you back?"

There was no way she was going to go into the trauma she'd gone through when she'd been choked to the brink of death only to be locked in a dark, damp basement room with no windows. The physical abuse was excruciating, but the psychological terror had been so much worse. She'd been trapped for endless hours, with nothing to do but think about Chip returning to finish what he'd started. He'd made it clear when he'd thrown her in there that he had every intention of returning to kill her. A shudder ran throughout her body. She knew beyond a shadow of doubt that she would never be able to shake the feeling of desperation and the sinking dread that came over her whenever she was forced to be in a dark, wet enclosed space. But she refused to go into all that. It wasn't the time or the place—and it definitely wasn't something she was comfortable sharing with a man she'd known for less than a day. On the other hand, though, she wasn't going to lie to Thad.

"I just can't stand to be in small, enclosed, dark places," she finally admitted. It was the truth. She'd just omitted the reason behind her fears.

He leaned back to look down at her, his smile gentle and caring. "It's okay. If it bothers you that much, we won't use the root cellar. We'll move on to plan B."

Relief flooded her. "And what's plan B?"

"The toolshed. It's not quite as good against thermal imaging...but we're not even sure that's what our attacker is using. Besides, the logs should be thick enough to hide our heat signature if that is what he's using and still give us some protection from a high-powered rifle slug." Turning her toward a path that disappeared into a cluster of birch trees, he slid his arm around her waist as she hobbled to their shelter. "Blane should be here in an hour or two with the horses, and we'll be back at his place in time for breakfast."

Thankfully, he didn't press her for a more detailed explanation of her reluctance to enter the cellar and she was grateful for his compassion. "Thank you," she murmured.

Thad gave her a gentle hug and remained silent as they entered the toolshed, then stationed himself at the door to keep watch while Carrie sank to the dirt floor. Leaning back against the wall, she rested her head against the rough-hewn logs of the small building. She hated feeling anxious and on edge, but she hated even more showing her weaknesses to anyone—especially a man. It gave him even more ways and means to take advantage of her, above and beyond exploiting her physical limitations. The only consolation in her current situation was that if she had to rely on a man for her well-being, she was thankful that it was Thad Hanson. So far, he'd been unfailingly kind and courteous. He hadn't acted as if he thought of her as incompetent because of her phobia, nor had he given any indication that he viewed her anxiety as a sign of her inferiority. Her ex-boyfriend had relished any opportunity to make her feel inadequate. It was as if he had to tear her down to make himself feel superior.

But all that stopped when Chip had been sentenced to twenty years in prison for attempting to murder her. Chip was gone now—not just from her life but from the world, since he lost his life in prison in a fight with another inmate. But although the physical injuries she sustained from his cruelty had healed, the mental scars ran much deeper. She glanced down at her tightly clenched fists and scrunched her eyes shut. In fact, they ran so deep, she was afraid they might never heal.

Someone or something was moving around out in the clearing. Thad clicked off the safety on his rifle as he glanced over at Carrie. She'd fallen asleep not long after she'd leaned back against the shed's back wall and he hated to wake her, but if they needed to bug out quickly it would be a lot better if she was already awake and ready to go.

"Carrie?" he whispered softly as he squatted down beside her. She stirred but didn't open her eyes. "Carrie, wake up."

"Don't tell me we have to run again," she murmured. "That's not what I want to hear."

Under different circumstances, he might have laughed, but their current situation was no laughing matter. And it seemed more likely than not that they really would have to run. "We've got company. I can't be sure if it's Drone Jerk chasing us or an animal foraging for food."

Her eyes instantly popped open and she

sat up to stare at him. "Could it possibly be your brother?"

"I don't think so," he said, shaking his head. "The sounds are coming from the wrong direction." He carefully looked out through the crack of the partially opened door. "Get your gun ready, and don't hesitate to shoot whatever comes through the door."

"You're going out there?" Her alarm was evident in the tone of her voice, making him feel like a complete jerk for leaving her.

"I'm not going far," he assured her. "But I need to check out what's rummaging around. If it *is* the guy chasing us, I don't want to run the risk of him sneaking up on us or my brother walking into an ambush."

He watched her draw her gun from the pocket of her insulated vest. "Let me know it's you before you open the door," she said, releasing the safety on her Glock. "I don't want to shoot you by mistake."

"And believe me when I say that I truly appreciate that," he said, grinning. He took a deep breath and reached to open the door. "I'll be right back."

"Thad?" she said, stopping him as she scrambled to her feet. When he turned back, she added, "Please, be careful."

He gave her a quick nod. "That's my plan."

Slipping silently through the doorway, he cut through the woods behind the root cellar. If this really was their assailant and not a wild animal, then it seemed he didn't care that he was making enough noise to be heard all the way down in Eagle Fork, a little over twenty miles away.

As he moved closer to the root cellar, he could hear muffled curses emanating from the interior of the earthen structure. Just as he suspected, it was the shooter, still determinedly trying to find them and put an end to them once and for all. Thad turned and quietly retraced his steps back to the toolshed. It would be in their best interest if he and Carrie started down the trail and intercepted Blane somewhere along the way up to meet them. If they could reach him before he got to the clearing, maybe they could keep the trigger-happy stalker from following them back to his part of the mountain.

"Carrie, it's me," Thad said, keeping his voice low. Hoping she heard him and didn't start firing off rounds, he opened the shed door and slipped inside. "We need to go. He's in the root cellar, and he's definitely not in a good mood."

"How are we going to get past him?" she asked, hobbling over to stand beside him.

"We'll go through the woods and start down the trail my brother will use to come up here," he said as they left the shed. "We'll meet up with Blane along the way and be eating breakfast before this guy realizes we aren't up here on the mountain with him."

"I hope you're right, Thad."

Her soft voice saying his name sent a warm feeling zinging around inside his chest, like a pinball in an arcade game. He couldn't help feeling annoyed with himself. He *did* find her attractive, and he admired her courage, but they were being chased by some guy trying to kill them, and he was going all mushy inside just from her saying his name?

Not the time or the circumstances, Hanson! Get a grip. The lady isn't interested in you and nothing could come of it even if she was. Remember? Just like she doesn't do dark enclosed places, you don't do relationships. She needed him to get her off the mountain, not go all moon-eyed over her and get them both shot.

While they headed through the woods, he tried to get his mind off of his beautiful companion and back on the matter at hand.

By his estimation they should meet up with Blane and the horses in approximately thirty minutes. And that was just fine with him. The longer he was with Carrie, the bigger the chance he would end up sticking his size thirteen boot in his mouth and prove that he was every bit the awkward, backwoods, country bumpkin his ex-girlfriend had accused him of being.

Not long after the sun cleared the peaks to the west of Blane's part of the ranch, Thad lifted Carrie down from the saddle on the big chestnut mare Blane had brought for her, then watched her take a step to test her ankle. "How's it feel?" he asked, taking hold of her elbow in case pain or weakness caused the joint to give way.

"Surprisingly, I think it's better," she said, taking a couple of steps. "Apparently resting it when we were waiting for your brother at the shed and then riding the horses instead of hiking down the mountain helped."

"It's nice that things worked out for a change," he said, relieved they successfully made it down the mountain without further incident.

"It certainly is," Carrie agreed, smiling.

Turning toward his brother, she extended her hand. "Thank you for the ride on your gorgeous horse, Blane. I'm glad I got to meet you."

"It was my pleasure." Thad ground his back teeth when his brother shot him a knowing grin as he shook Carrie's hand a little longer than was necessary. "I just wish it had been under better circumstances, Game Warden Caldwell."

She nodded. "I do, too. And please, call me Carrie."

Blane's eyes sparkled with humor when he nodded. "I set up the timer on the coffee maker before I left this morning, and there should be a fresh pot of coffee, *Carrie*. If you'd like to go on inside and grab a cup, Thad and I will be in as soon as we finish taking care of the horses. We'll have breakfast before I take you over to his place. And when my foreman went over to check out the damage to Sean's place, he picked up the things you and Thad had to leave behind. Your phone and clothes are on the couch in the great room."

"Thank you. I think I'll take you up on that coffee. And it will definitely be nice to change into my own clothes," she said, handing the mare's reins to Thad before she carefully climbed the steps to enter the back door.

Thad followed Blane as they led the horses into the barn and tied them to a hitching post. As sure as the sun rose in the east each morning, Blane was going to interrogate him about the time he'd spent with Carrie and the degree of his interest in her. He couldn't stop the interrogation…but he could stall it by asking his brother about something else. "So you sent someone over to secure Sean's place and board up the window in the kitchen?" he asked as he removed the saddles from his and Carrie's horses to start brushing them down. "How bad is it?"

"After I got off the phone when you called to tell me that you and your lady had to bug out, I got hold of Jake and told him to go over there to take care of it and pick up your and Carrie's things," Blane answered. "He called me just before I took off to ride up to the lodge and said the window over the kitchen sink was broken. He got one of Sean's men to help him nail a piece of plywood over it until he can go down to Eagle Fork later this morning to get a replacement window pane. He'll head over there this afternoon and get it installed. It will be as good as new when

Sean and Bailey get back from their honeymoon this evening."

"Thanks. Tell him to have Sally at the Rancher's General Store put it all on my bill." He huffed out an exasperated breath. "And just for the record, Carrie is not my lady. She's a state conservation officer and that's it. End of story."

"Word on the street is she's single," Blane advised happily, ignoring Thad's dark scowl.

"By 'street' you mean the gossip around the firehouse," he muttered, leading his and Carrie's mounts to their stalls. Like most small towns, there was always a place where men gathered to visit, speculate on everything from the weather to the price of cattle and swap stories about what was going on in the community. In Eagle Fork the fire station was that place.

Sighing heavily, he finished giving each of the horses a big scoop of oats and a flake of hay, then walked back to where Blane waited expectantly by the tack room door. Hoping to head off any further speculation, Thad glared at him. "Yes, she's single, but she isn't interested in me any more than I'm interested in her."

Blane threw back his head and laughed

until he had to wipe tears from his eyes. "Do-little, you crack me up. Do you honestly think you can make me believe you haven't noticed how pretty she is?"

"Drop it, Blane. I'm not blind. I know drop-dead gorgeous when I see it. But even if she did give me a second glance—which, by the way, she hasn't and won't—you know I have a lousy track record with women. She and I are just better off being friends and that's that."

Blane's grin disappeared as he stared at Thad for several long seconds before he shook his head. "Thad, you have to let go of what Missy said to you. She was a shallow, self-centered, immature girl who used you as a diversion for her loneliness and insecurities while she was away from home."

"So now you're Sigmund Freud?"

"When she was in high school, she was a big fish in a little pond," his brother went on as if he hadn't commented at all. "She was popular and got a lot of attention from all the boys. But when she started college she found out she wasn't nearly as big of a deal on campus as she expected to be. You were enamored with her, and she absorbed all of that attention and adoration like a sponge."

"That's ancient history," Thad said, wishing his brother would leave his past social experiences where they belonged. In the past.

"It obviously isn't if you're letting it keep you from pursuing a relationship with someone else."

"Thanks for your keen observation, big brother. But instead of focusing on my love life, why don't you focus on your own?" Thad shot back. "When was the last time you took a woman out?"

"We're not talking about me," Blane said, shrugging. "You're the one hanging out with a pretty lady game warden."

"We're not hanging out. I'm just trying to keep her alive while she's here on our mountain," he said pointedly. "As soon as she gets back to the WGFD station in Eagle Fork, she'll start her investigation, coordinate with the other law enforcement agencies and catch this trigger-happy idiot. Meanwhile, I fully expect for things around here to go back to being business as usual. The end."

"Since the trouble started when she showed up, I'm assuming that she's this jerk's main target?" Blane asked.

Thad shrugged. "It seems that way. She thinks it might be one of the hunters from a poaching ring she busted a little over a year ago up close to the Montana line."

"I get the idea you aren't convinced."

"Not at all." Rubbing the tension at the back of his neck, he shook his head. "This feels a little too personal for it to be some guy she arrested for poaching. When I showed up at Whisper Lake yesterday afternoon, he was tormenting her with a drone, and it was like he was playing some kind of psychological game with her. He'd keep shooting at her, but he'd always miss." He clenched his jaw against his building anger. "And believe me, as close as that drone was to her, he had to work hard not to hit her."

"Sounds like he wants to terrorize her before he ends the game. That *does* sound more personal than just some guy she arrested trying to get even with her." Frowning, Blane shook his head. "What kind of man does that to a woman? Or anybody else for that matter?"

"I don't know, nor have I been able to figure out how he knew to look for her here, but I'm going to do my best to keep him from causing her any more anxiety while she's on this ranch."

As they left the barn and started toward

the house, Blane asked, "Where's her WGFD truck?"

"Unless this guy took it, it's still parked at the trailhead west of Whisper Valley." He stopped on the back porch before they entered the house, wanting to end the discussion before stepping inside. Carrie had already been through enough over the past eighteen hours, and she was completely exhausted. He didn't want to add his concerns to the worries she already had. "When I take her down there to get her truck, I intend to follow her into town. I don't trust this guy not to have tampered with the truck. Or maybe we'll find that he has parked somewhere along the road, waiting to intercept her on her way back to the station. I'm going to personally ensure that she gets home safe."

Blane's smile was one of complete agreement. "I'd be disappointed in you if you didn't, little brother."

SIX

When Thad parked his quad-cab truck next to the dark green WGFD pickup, Carrie reached for the door handle to let herself out. "Thanks for the ride and..." She stopped when he placed his hand on her arm.

"This guy could be hanging around waiting for you to come back," he cautioned. "Let me check things out first with your truck to make sure he hasn't messed with anything."

Carrie shook her head and opened the passenger door. "Don't worry about me. I'll be fine. When I was in college, my father and brothers made sure I learned how to do a safety check on a vehicle. My training as a peace officer covered that, as well."

She didn't tell him that her knowledge pertaining to checking a vehicle for tampering had been due to her family's concerns after she'd recovered from Chip's attack. They had enrolled her in defense classes for women who had been stalked or in abusive relationships. In addition to self-defense, the courses had covered being aware of danger in her surroundings, as well as how to look for and identify vehicle tampering, tracking and explosive devices.

"I don't like you being out in the open like this," he said, following her as she got down to look at the undercarriage for foreign objects, cut brake lines or a punctured power steering fluid hose. As she got to her feet, he looked around. "Drone Jerk could be hiding behind any one of the thousands of trees and bushes surrounding the area, just waiting for his chance to shoot at you."

His quietly spoken statement made her realize that, by following her so closely around the truck, he'd been placing himself between her and possible danger. Touched by his concern, she put her hand on his arm. "Thad, I can't thank you enough for all that you've done for me over the past twenty-four hours, but I'll be fine now. Really. And there's so much I need to do. Once I get back to the warden station, I'll check in again with WGFD and all the law enforcement agencies to see if the APB and BOLO I sent last night from your brother's house produced any results. Then I'll start investigating the men involved in the poaching ring and have some of my fellow WGFD officers assigned to that district bring them in for questioning as to their whereabouts yesterday and last night."

He stared at her for what seemed like an eternity before he finally nodded. "I'm sorry you had problems here on Cougar Mountain. But you're welcome back anytime," he assured with a warm smile. When she opened the driver's door on her truck and slid behind the steering wheel, he waited until she'd buckled her seat belt and reached to close the door. "Drive carefully and I'll see you at the WGFD station."

She frowned. "You're following me to Eagle Fork?"

"Of course."

"Why? No one has bothered my service vehicle, nor has anyone shot at me in almost eight hours. I told you I'd be just fine. I'm hoping whoever it was has moved on."

"Maybe so, but maybe not," he said stubbornly. "After the way this guy came after us so many times last night, I want to know for sure that you made it safe and sound to your office." Without giving her a chance to protest further, he closed the driver's door on the WGFD truck and walked over to climb back into his vehicle.

As she started the pickup and drove toward the main road, she glanced in the rearview mirror to see his bigger truck following at a safe distance behind. Shaking her head, she fumed at the man's obstinacy. But if he wanted to waste his time following her back to her office that was his business, and there was really nothing she could do to stop him. Determined to ignore him, she turned her thoughts to the investigation that lay ahead of her to bring the perpetrator to justice. When he threatened her and Thad with a deadly weapon, he'd committed a class five felony and needed to be stopped before he killed someone. But even as she tried to concentrate on the next steps, all she could think about was the good-looking veterinarian following her.

She sighed and wondered what on earth was wrong with her. She couldn't stop the butterflies flapping around in her stomach whenever she looked in the rearview mirror to see his white truck behind her. She'd sworn off men seven years ago and that was that.

No "if, ands or buts" about it, she wasn't interested. Not even a little bit.

Distracted by her disturbing thoughts concerning the extremely kind and caring man following her, it took a moment for her to realize that the shiny black truck with a heavy-duty chrome brush guard over the grill coming toward her was inching closer and closer to the broken white center lines on the asphalt highway. It was probably some kid texting his girlfriend, she decided when the driver drifted back into his own lane. But whoever was behind the wheel had no sooner moved back into his own lane than he swerved into her lane and headed straight for her.

Time seemed to stop, along with her heart, as the black truck not only bore down on her but sped up. If she swerved onto the shoulder, she worried that the heavy rain from the night before might have softened the ground to the point it would collapse beneath the weight of the truck, flipping it into the deep ditch below. But if she didn't do something soon, she was going to be involved in a head-on collision.

With no time to second-guess herself, she jerked the steering wheel to the right and bounced along the unstable shoulder. "Dear Lord, please help me!"

* * *

Thad was certain he lost ten years off his life as he watched the black truck cross the center line and barrel down the road toward the WGFD truck. Helpless to do anything, he was a trapped audience watching the danger play out in front of him.

Dear God, please keep Carrie safe in Your care!

Just when he was certain the black vehicle was going to crash head-on into her truck, she steered it off the road onto the shoulder and came to a shuddering stop. The black truck continued on and barely missed crashing into him before it roared away.

Stomping on the brake, he brought the dually to a sliding halt, barely waiting for the truck to stop before he threw the door open and hit the ground running. As soon as he got to the driver's door on the WGFD truck, he stopped dead in his tracks. Carrie was leaning forward with her forehead resting against the steering wheel.

He carefully opened the door and started to reach for her, but stopped. He didn't dare move her because he wasn't sure if she'd sustained a serious injury to her neck or back. Not to mention, with the way the truck was sitting on the edge of the shoulder, if she moved around too much, her truck might slide on down into the deep ditch.

"Carrie, are you all right? Come on, talk to me. I need to get you out of the truck, but first I have to know if you're hurt and where."

She slowly raised her head to reveal tears flowing down her unnaturally pale cheeks. It bothered him to see any woman cry, but the sight of Carrie's tears just about tore him in two and made him feel completely inept. She was terrified and he couldn't do anything to help her. "I-I'm not…h-hurt. H-he could…h-have killed…b-both of us," she sobbed, her hands shaking as she pushed her long hair away from her face. Turning toward him, she reached out. That was all the prompting he needed to take her into his arms and lift her out of the driver's seat. Cradling her to his chest, he'd just taken a step back from the truck when, as he'd feared, it rolled side over side down the embankment into the deep ditch below.

"It's going to be okay," he said, as he carried her to his truck. "You're out of danger and safe now." He never knew what to do or say when a woman became emotional, and he hoped he was saying the right thing to calm her nerves and make her feel better. Handing her one of the bottles of water he always kept in the truck, he reached for his cell phone clipped to his belt. "I'm going to call 9-1-1. The Eagle Fork Police will need to process the scene, and the Fire and Rescue Squad can check you to see if you need to be transported to the hospital in Cheyenne."

After placing the emergency call, he watched her take a deep breath, swipe at her eyes and shake her head. "I was just frightened beyond words from seeing that truck come at me. But really, Thad, I'm fine physically. As soon as I get my nerves under control, I'll be okay emotionally, as well."

The sound of her soft voice saying his name robbed him of breath. "I, uh…" He stopped to clear his suddenly rusty throat, then tried again. "I'd still feel better if you'd let the EMTs check you out. My brother, Levi, is on duty and he's one of the best paramedics in Wyoming." He pointed to her foot. "While he's at it he could even check your ankle."

"All right, but I'm telling you I'm fine," she insisted, taking a drink from the water bottle. Replacing the cap, she asked, "Did you happen to see the driver's face? Was it the same guy? Drone Jerk?"

Thad regretfully shook his head. "I'm not sure. All of the windows, including the windshield, were heavily tinted. I couldn't tell who was behind the wheel. And before you ask, the license plate was covered with mud. There was no way I could get his tag numbers."

She sighed. "It probably wouldn't have been much of a lead, anyway. The truck or the plates could have been stolen."

"That would be my guess," he agreed. The distant sound of sirens interrupted his thoughts. "Sounds like the cavalry is about five minutes out."

"Do you think this will take long?" Her flawless complexion was a healthier color, and her hands only trembled slightly when she pulled the band holding her hair loose and finger combed the golden strands, then drew it back up into a ponytail and secured it with the stretchy red elastic. "I'd really like to get back to my station and find out if there were any hits on the APB I put out last night."

The Fire and Rescue ambulance followed the two police cars as they pulled up along the road beside Thad's truck, blocking both lanes of the highway. "Levi, I need you to take a look at Carrie," Thad said as his brother walked toward his truck carrying an emergency bag.

"What happened?" his brother asked, setting the pack down to step up to the open passenger door where Carrie sat sideways on the seat.

"Really, I'm fine," she tried to assure them. "I really don't think this is necessary, but if it will ease Thad's mind, go ahead."

Thad groaned when his brother shot an irritating grin over his shoulder at him. "Thad has a tendency to overreact," Levi agreed, sounding sympathetic as he reached for his stethoscope and blood pressure cuff. "I can tell you from past experience that he won't shut up until I pronounce you fit as a fiddle, so I guess we should probably go along with him for now. He seemed to be especially concerned about your ankle when he called dispatch. Is it all right with you if I check it out?"

Half of the reason Levi was one of the best paramedics in the state of Wyoming was due to his ability to read people and meet them on their level, ease their fears and assess their condition at the same time. He always managed to find the perfect way to get an accident victim to relax and listen to him.

Rolling his eyes and shaking his head as Levi got Carrie to agree to let him examine her ankle, Thad pointed over at the deputy sheriff taking pictures of the WGFD truck upside-down in the ditch. "Carrie can fill you in on what happened while I make sure Rod has a tow truck on the way," he said, turning toward the deputy sheriff.

"How's it going, Doc?" Deputy Sheriff Jenkins asked, using the nickname Thad had been given when his teammates on the high school football team learned he wanted to be a veterinarian. He and Rod Jenkins had gone to school together, played football together and been good friends for as long as he could remember.

"As you can see," he said, gesturing to the pickup in the ditch, "things have been better." He hooked his thumbs in his belt loops as he slid his hands in the front pockets of his jeans and looked down at the truck, lying with its tires pointed to the sky like a turtle on its back at the bottom of the embankment. His heart stalled at the sight of the cab's smashed roof and broken windows. He had to take a deep breath to ease the tightness in his chest. Only the grace of God had kept Carrie from becoming a statistic. *Thank you, Lord, for watching over her and keeping her safe.*

"Dispatch said the new game warden barely escaped a head-on crash." Rod took another picture of the truck with his cell phone. "She also said you saw the whole thing."

Thad nodded. "I was behind her and I don't think this was an accident." He told his friend what had transpired over the past twenty-four hours. "By the way," he said when he finished, "did you call Roberts' Towing to pull the truck out of the ditch or do you want me to give D.J. a call?"

"I'll take care of it, Doc," Rod said, reaching for the mic clipped to his shoulder. "I'll call dispatch and have Vera get hold of D.J." He grinned. "She'll jump at the chance to talk to him. She's been crushing on him since we were all in middle school."

Thad smiled and nodded. "Thanks for taking care of that." He turned to go back to where Levi stood, talking to Carrie. He knew it wasn't any of his business and she'd be the first one to tell him so, but Thad couldn't walk away when the danger against her was still ongoing. He was going to stick to her like superglue until this guy was caught and brought to justice.

* * *

Exhaustion settled over Carrie as Thad drove them into the parking lot of her WGFD station just outside the small town of Eagle Fork. She needed at least eight hours of uninterrupted sleep, but as tired as she was, sleep was going to have to wait until she filed her reports with her regional supervisor and updated her APB and BOLO with the newest information about being forced off the road.

"Thank you for giving me a ride, Thad," she said, when he parked the truck. She glanced down at her tightly fisted hands in her lap. Forcing herself to relax, she uncurled her fingers and took a deep cleansing breath. Now that she was back at her station, she could escalate the investigation and hopefully regain her equilibrium in the process. But he'd done so much more than just drive her to the station. She felt compelled to try to put her gratitude into words. "Most of all, thank you for saving my life so many times." So much had happened in just over twenty-four hours. It felt surreal, almost as if it had all been an extremely vivid nightmare. "I wouldn't even be here if you hadn't…"

"Don't think about it," he said gently, reaching over to take her hand in his much larger one. The warmth and tenderness of his touch sent a wave of longing zinging through her that she didn't understand and wasn't sure she wanted to. "God protected both of us, Carrie."

"Yes, He did." *Thank You, dear Lord, for sending this man when I needed him most. And thank You for keeping both of us safe.*

"I thought this was a one-person station. Do you have someone working with you?" Thad asked suddenly as he stared through the windshield at the log building nestled back in the lush grove of Douglas fir trees.

When she looked up, she gasped at the sight of the front door standing partially open. "I closed and locked that door when I left yesterday. And you're right—this is a one-person station. No one else has access."

"Stay in the truck," he ordered, releasing her hand and opening the driver's door.

"Not on your life," she muttered stubbornly. Before he could stop her, she opened the passenger door and jumped down from the truck. As she headed for the entrance of the building, Thad took hold of her arm to stop her.

"Let me check it out before you go barreling inside. There could be someone or something in there that won't take kindly to being startled."

"Thad…"

"At least let me go ahead of you," he said, stepping in front of her. "If a bear or mountain lion managed to get inside, they might still be in there."

She knew he was only trying to keep her safe, but she wasn't helpless. It was her job to deal with nuisance animals as well as people breaking the law, and she'd been well trained to handle both. Not giving her the chance to do anything but follow him, she stayed behind him until he cleared the doorway and stopped just inside the office area. When she stepped around him, the sight of her normally neat and orderly station completely trashed caused her to cover her mouth with both hands to keep from crying out in horror. The locked file cabinets had been pried open and the contents dumped on the floor. Every picture, poster and framed certificate had been torn from the wall, the frames and glass shattered. And every drawer in her desk had been emptied on top of the piles of debris. But the sight of the picture of her and her family that she kept sitting on top of her desk nearly destroyed what little composure she had left.

The glass of the frame had been smashed, but then the photo had been removed and torn into quarters. The person responsible had then used a permanent marker to draw a big black X over her face. Her knees threatened to buckle, and she would have fallen if Thad hadn't reached out to put his arm around her waist to keep her from crumpling into a heap on the floor.

"Wh-who would do this? And wh-why?" she asked, not really expecting an answer.

"As enraged as he was up there on the mountain at the old lodge site when we gave him the slip, Drone Jerk gets my vote," Thad said, shaking his head. "He had plenty of time to get here and trash the place while we were at Blane's. And when we met him on our way here, he'd probably just left and was heading back to the mountain to look for us again."

She nodded. "Since the glass in the front door isn't broken, he probably gained entry through the back door of the cabin. It's sheltered from view by the trees so one could see him from the road." A sudden thought had her breaking away from Thad to take off down the short hall on shaky legs to her living quarters at the back of the cabin. Flinging open the door, she couldn't begin to find the words to describe how devastated she was by the sight before her. If she'd thought her office was bad, the living area of the small cabin was even worse. There wasn't a piece of furniture in the living room that hadn't been slashed or smashed, and the cabinets in the small kitchenette had been emptied. Broken glasses and dishes were scattered all over the counters, and even the food she'd had in the refrigerator had been thrown onto the tile floor. This was an act of pure hatred and rage and went beyond any retaliation for arresting someone for poaching. *Dear God, please grant me the strength and wisdom to deal with all of this. I need Your guidance, Lord.*

As she stared at the tatters and fragments of her life, the tightness in her chest began to ease, replaced by a calm resolve. It was going to be all right. It wasn't going to be easy to deal with this latest violation of her privacy, but she stiffened her spine and squared her shoulders. She was alive and unharmed, and what the perp had destroyed were just material things. There wasn't anything he'd torn up that couldn't be replaced.

She started toward her bedroom. "I need to see if my clothes…"

Thad gently placed his hand on her shoulder, and his voice was quiet and comforting when he spoke. "It's probably not a good idea to go in there. I doubt that it's any better than this."

She stared at him for a moment as her law enforcement training kicked in. "You're right. Could you please call the police, while I call my regional supervisor?" When he nodded, she pointed toward the front of the cabin. "We should make our calls from your truck. This is a crime scene, and until the crime scene techs get it processed, the less time we spend in here the better."

After they got back into the cab of his truck, while Thad called Deputy Sheriff Jenkins, Carrie reported in with her regional supervisor, Senior Game Warden Arthur Sullivan. After explaining everything that had happened in the past two days, he put her on paid administrative leave and advised her that he was sending someone in to replace her until authorities caught whoever was responsible for the attacks.

"Please, Warden Sullivan, I'd like to be in on catching whoever this is," she argued. "I can't be part of the investigation if I'm on leave, sir."

"It's obvious you're his target. I can't take

the chance on leaving you in charge of the station and have this guy continue to come after you," he said, sounding so authoritative she wanted to scream. "I don't want you getting hurt or worse. It's for your safety, Carrie. As of this minute, you are officially on leave until this is resolved."

"But, sir…"

"I'm sorry, Carrie, but that's my final word." His voice lost the formal tone when he added, "You're a good warden with a bright future at the WGFD. And before you assume I'm doing this because you're a woman, let me assure you, I'd make the same decision if a male warden was in the same situation." He paused before he finished. "Carrie, I promise that as soon as this is over and you're no longer being threatened, I'll make sure you're immediately reinstated in the Eagle Fork office. Or, if you'd like, there's a station coming open closer to where your folks live. I would be happy to assign you there."

Sighing, she knew it was futile to try changing his mind. "Thank you, sir. I'll look forward to hearing from you when the guilty party is caught and charged."

When she ended her call, she turned to find Thad carefully watching her from the driver's side of the truck. "I'm sorry. I didn't mean to eavesdrop, but I take it your boss isn't happy?" he said.

"Not at all." She stuffed her cell phone into her insulated vest and zipped the pocket closed. "He's worried about me and has put me on administrative leave until whoever keeps shooting at me is caught."

He reached out to take hold of her hand and give it a supportive squeeze. "Are you going back up north where your folks are?"

"I don't want to, but I don't think I'm going to have a choice." Hearing the sound of sirens, she knew in just a matter of a few hours she'd be on her way to her parents' ranch up by Sheridan. "The warden who'll be replacing me will need the living quarters, and I doubt I can find a place to rent short-term in Eagle Fork. But what I'd really like to do is stay here and start my own investigation to catch this guy."

"You're more than welcome to stay on the Cougar Mountain Ranch," he offered. "But are you sure doing your own investigation is a good idea?"

"I've already put you and your family through enough." She shook her head. "I can't keep imposing on you, putting all of you in more danger. I'll just have to figure out how to work on the case some other way."

"It's not an imposition in the least," he insisted. "And don't worry about my family. We've been defending our mountain and the people on it, as well as the animals, for over a hundred and fifty years. Besides, when he threatened me, that put him on the entire Hanson family radar." He grinned. "You take on one of us, you get us all."

Tempted by his offer in spite of herself, she murmured more to herself than to him, "I'd really like to stay close and keep up with what's going on, but I've been enough of a problem."

"You haven't been a problem, Carrie. And there's no reason for you to think you can't stay on the ranch. My place has four bedrooms, each with a private bathroom. There's plenty of room." He shrugged one shoulder. "You can use my computer for your investigation."

"But there's no telling how long it'll be before this guy is caught," she argued. "I can't just mooch off of you indefinitely."

"Then don't—if you'd like, you can be my assistant when I'm working with the animals."

"Thad, I appreciate your offer, and I would absolutely love helping you with the animals, but…"

He gave her a smile that caused her heart to skip a beat. "All you have to do is say 'yes,' Carrie. It's as easy as that."

Staring into the warmth of his dark brown eyes, she found herself nodding her acceptance. She hoped she wasn't making a mistake, but if she stayed in the area instead of being several hundred miles away, she might be able to help bring her assailant to justice. She only hoped she wouldn't be bringing more trouble to Cougar Mountain than the Hanson family was prepared to handle.

SEVEN

After showing Carrie to the room she would be using while she stayed with him, Thad closed the door and walked down the hallway to his office. Since all of her clothes had been ripped to shreds by the vandal, they'd made a quick stop at the bank for her to make a withdrawal then another at the Rancher's General Store to pick up some replacements. While she put her new clothes away, he intended to call a meeting with his three brothers.

He was apprehensive about Carrie conducting her own investigation. To his way of thinking, it was way too dangerous with few, if any rewards. Any evidence she obtained could be dismissed by the courts as biased and inadmissible. And undertaking the investigation would just put her in harm's way.

He took a deep breath and slowly released it. He realized she was a trained officer. Unfortunately, the way this guy was going after her, her training didn't do a lot to put his mind at ease. Even the biggest, toughest law officer could be ambushed. But at least by having her stay at the ranch, he could be her backup and make sure she stayed as safe as possible. And, he'd have help. He had three older brothers who would be more than happy to put the perpetrator in his place for disturbing the tranquility on Cougar Mountain.

Dialing his oldest brother's number, it rang a couple of times before Sean picked up. "Hey, little brother, I hear you've been having a few problems," his brother stated as a greeting.

"Yeah, it's been real…interesting around here the past couple of days," he admitted. "And I'm sorry about your house being damaged."

"It's all good. Blane had one of his men fix it before Bailey and I got home from the airport this afternoon. If he hadn't called to tell me about it, I never would have realized it had happened." Sean laughed. "You know I'd be the last one to place blame on anyone. If you'll remember, I had a hand in getting a few windows shattered at Blane's and Levi's places when I was guarding Bailey. So you might say I had it coming." Last year, Sean had been asked by the FBI to negotiate the release of a woman being held captive by a bank robber, then he'd been tasked with keeping her safe when the robber escaped custody. The robber had chased them to the mountain, with multiple attacks along the way. On the bright side, by the time the man was caught and brought to justice, Sean and Bailey had fallen for each other, and now Thad had a new sister-in-law.

"I know for certain nobody blamed you for that, but I'm glad Blane's hired hand made the repairs to yours so you didn't have to deal with it when you returned home." Thad hesitated a moment before he asked, "I know you and Bailey just got back from your honeymoon, and I'm really sorry to ask this of you, but would you mind coming over tomorrow morning after breakfast? I need to meet with you, Blane and Levi to bring you all up to speed on what happened today and enlist your help to keep Carrie safe."

"Do you need us to come over now?" Sean asked, yawning.

"No. It's quiet for now and I have all of the hired hands posted around the house and barns. We should be okay tonight."

"All right. I'll be there in the morning on one condition." Thad could hear the humor in his brother's voice.

"Name it," he shot back.

Sean yawned into the phone again. "Have a pot of coffee ready. I've got a case of jet lag that won't quit."

Thad laughed. "That's what you get for going all the way to Hawaii for your honeymoon."

"I told Bailey we would honeymoon anywhere she wanted, and she chose Hawaii." He chuckled. "And if Bailey wants it, you know that I'm going to try to make it happen."

Thad laughed. "When the love bug bit you, he got you real good, bro."

"I'm just waiting for the day he takes a bite out of you," his brother shot back.

"Don't hold your breath, big brother." Before Sean could needle him any more, Thad quickly added, "Get some sleep, and rest assured I'll keep the coffee coming tomorrow morning."

When he ended the call, he phoned Blane and Levi and, after setting the meeting up with them, went into the kitchen to stare into the refrigerator, wondering what on earth he could offer Carrie for supper. They'd missed lunch due to answering questions and giving their statements to the various branches of law enforcement that had shown up at the WGFD office, and he hadn't given picking up some groceries a second thought when they'd stopped at the Rancher's General Store for Carrie's clothes. Now his stomach was beginning to grumble about being neglected.

"What are you trying to find?" Carrie asked, walking up beside him to look around the door of the refrigerator. "You're staring in here like it holds the mysteries of the universe."

"I'm really sorry, but I'm afraid I don't have a whole lot to choose from for supper." He let loose a frustrated sigh. "Besides a carton of eggs and a half gallon of milk, all I've got is some deli roast beef, cheese, whole wheat bread and a jar of grape jelly." He looked at the milk carton, then grimaced. "Uh, scratch the milk off that list. It expired three days ago."

"You really don't cook a lot, do you?" she asked, giving him an amused smile. "What do you have in the pantry?"

"To tell you the truth, I'm not really sure." He rubbed the back of his neck while heat crept up from his collar to spread over his cheeks. Until now, keeping a well-stocked pantry and being able to cook really hadn't been a high priority. "I, uh, don't eat at home very often."

"Why?" she asked, pointing to the doorway on the far side of the kitchen. "Is that the pantry?" When he nodded, she walked over and disappeared inside for a few moments before returning with two different types of chips, a jar of dill pickle spears and a couple of cans of soup.

"Well, my clinic in Eagle Fork is open from seven in the morning until five in the afternoon, five days a week. Then after the clinic closes I go out on ranch calls for several hours, and on Saturdays when the clinic is closed, I work at the rehab center." He gave her a one shoulder shrug. "I'm hardly ever home in time to eat, much less with time to spare for cooking something from scratch. I usually grab whatever the special is at Maggie's Diner when I'm in town, and around here I throw a frozen pizza in the oven if I have one, make a sandwich if there's something in the fridge to slap between two slices of bread or eat a bowl of cereal."

"What do you do on Sundays?" she asked as she placed the items from the pantry on the kitchen island.

"Sean's wife is real big on keeping all of us connected and close." He couldn't help but smile. The entire Hanson clan loved Bailey and they had been more than happy to welcome her into their family. "Every Sunday evening she cooks a big meal and we all get together to eat and catch up. We share what's been going on for the week, discuss who needs help around their section of the mountain and give each other advice whether we want it or not."

"Bailey sounds like a wonderful person," Carrie said, smiling. "I hope I get to meet her sometime."

"You'll meet her Sunday evening when we all get together for supper," he said, nodding.

"Are you sure your family won't mind me joining in?" she asked, looking unsure. "I don't want to intrude on your time together."

"No one will mind at all." He grinned. "Bailey would take a strip off my hide if I didn't include you. Believe me, she's the best, and when it comes to cooking she's top-notch. She loves to feed people."

"I'm looking forward to getting to know her. And it's wonderful that you have one good meal a week. Otherwise, you eat worse than a teenager, Dr. Hanson," she said, laughing as she opened the cans of soup to pour into a saucepan and place on the stove. Taking the bread from the bread box on the counter, she asked, "What do you want on your roast beef and cheddar sandwich? Mustard? Mayo? Ketchup?"

"Plain is fine," he said, reaching into one of the cabinets beside the sink for a couple of plates. "Since the milk isn't an option, do you want water or should I make a pot of coffee?"

"How about both?" She handed him the bags of chips and jar of pickles to place on the table. "Water with our meal and coffee after? I found a package of cookies we could have for dessert."

"Awesome! Cookies are a favorite of mine. And a glass of water and cup of coffee are two things even I can't screw up." Happy to be able to do something useful toward their supper, he put the chips and pickles on the table, then turned to fill two glasses with ice water and start the coffee pot.

As he watched Carrie finish making her sandwich and bring their plates and bowls of soup to the table, he couldn't help but acknowledge how nice it was to have her in his kitchen—the two of them working together to fix their meal. He could get used to the easy companionship of having her in his home, in his life.

His heart stalled and he shook his head to dislodge the notion. She was here because of circumstances beyond either of their control and that was that. Once the trigger-happy jerk chasing them ended up in jail and life got back to normal, she would go her way and he would go back to taking care of all the animals—both wild and domestic—in Cougar County. And maybe if he told himself that was the way it should be enough times, he'd accept it, stop thinking about things that could never be and move on.

When the back door to the mudroom closed and Thad, accompanied by three tall, broad-shouldered men, walked into the kitchen the following morning, Carrie couldn't help but notice once again what a strong resemblance there was between the Hanson brothers. She'd noticed it when she met Blane and Levi and found Sean to be just like them. Although the four brothers had different shades of brown hair and varied a bit in height, they all had the same warm brown eyes and mischievous grin, making them remarkably handsome and charming in an attractive, cowboy way.

"You must be Carrie Caldwell," the only one she hadn't met said, stepping forward to shake her hand. "I'm Sean Hanson. My apologies that you had to meet all the rest of my brothers before you got to the good one."

"Hey, now," Blane said, laughing. Turning to give her a conspiratorial wink, he shook his head. "Don't listen to them, Carrie. They're all jealous because I'm the best looking of the Hanson bunch."

"Who in the name of Sam Hill are you trying to kid, Blane?" Grinning from ear to ear, Levi slapped his brother on the back. "You just confirmed what we've all suspected for years. You don't have anything in that hard head of yours but hot air."

Blane laughed. "Why do you think I wear my hat all the time? It keeps my head from deflating."

Carrie laughed until tears filled her eyes. Listening to the Hanson brothers was like listening to her own older brothers. Their jabs were always good-natured and came from a deep love for each other.

"Carrie, don't pay any attention to these guys," Thad said, shaking his head. "They're all a little wild, unpredictable and out of control most of the time. No telling what they'll say."

"That's what makes us fun." Levi grinned. "Don't let Dolittle fool you. He's a Cougar Mountain Maverick the same as the rest of us."

"Dolittle, like the fictional doctor?" she asked, beginning to catch on to their easy banter.

Blane nodded. "I hung that on him after he graduated from vet school."

"That makes sense, but who are the Cougar Mountain Mavericks?"

"We called ourselves that when we were kids, tearing around the mountain on horseback, looking for bad guys and hidden gold," Sean said, laughing. "Nobody bothered to tell us that the only gold found on Cougar Mountain was the tawny hides on the big cats the mountain was named for."

Thad walked over and handed Carrie and his brothers cups of coffee. "Now that you've embarrassed yourselves in front of the new Eagle Fork conservation officer, why don't we have a seat and I'll tell you what happened yesterday after we got to the WGFD station." They all remained standing until Thad set his coffee down and held a chair for her at the kitchen table. It wasn't until she was seated that the brothers pulled out chairs for themselves and joined her. Maybe good manners weren't a thing of the past after all, she thought fleetingly as she listened to Thad fill the men in on the chaotic scene at the WGFD station. "I've been placed on administrative leave until this is over and my assailant is behind bars," she added when he finished. "Since I'm off, I'm going to investigate some of the people I've arrested or fined for wildlife violations to see if I can identify the attacker."

"I'm not sure that's a good idea," Thad interjected.

The mood in the kitchen went from jovial to all business as the Hanson brothers digested what Thad and Carrie had told them and the gravity of the situation set in. "Just remember to turn over every lead you find to the authorities as soon as you find it. Let them follow up to see where it goes," Sean warned. "Otherwise, any evidence coming from you could be thrown out by a judge and the perp could walk."

"I have my superior at WGFD, the Department of Criminal Investigation and the Eagle Fork Sheriff's Department on speed dial,"

Carrie said, nodding. "I want to do this right, believe me. No one's more invested in making sure this guy gets locked away than me."

"Have you had any problems here on your part of the ranch, Thad?" Sean asked, taking a sip of his coffee.

Thad shook his head. "No—or at least, not yet. But there's a lot going on here most of the time with the quarter horse breeding program I'm starting and the rehab center. Not to mention all the people dropping by on the weekends to have me look at an animal outside of my office hours. Sneaking around here would be a lot harder."

"This dude probably isn't willing to risk somebody seeing what he's up to and being able to identify him in a lineup," Levi offered.

"That's what I think," Sean said thoughtfully. "The fewer people who are able to describe or identify him, the better off he is. But that doesn't necessarily mean he'll avoid coming around if there are other people here. Crowds offer some protective camouflage that would let him slip in unnoticed."

Levi nodded. "He could get lost in the crowd and be in and out of here with little or no notice."

"Watch your and Carrie's six, little brother,"

Blane warned. "Just because he hasn't bothered around here, doesn't mean he won't if he gets the chance."

"I can take a week off from the fire station," Levi offered. "I'll take the night watch."

"Good idea," Blane said, nodding. "I'll join you and we'll double-team this jerk like we did last year when Sean was protecting Bailey."

"I'll be here during the day to be your shadow," Sean said, sitting back in his chair. "Wherever you two go, I'll follow. If you go up to the rehab center or out to the stables, I'll tag along."

"Won't Bailey protest you being away from her?" Thad asked.

"I'm pretty sure she'll understand, after what we went through last Christmas," Sean said. Grinning, he shrugged. "Besides, Mom and Dad are coming back from Phoenix tomorrow and should be here for a week or two. I'll be surprised if Bailey and Mom aren't planning on redecorating another room in the house. All the better for me not to be underfoot for that."

"They were just here," Thad said, frowning. "Last thing I heard, they weren't coming back until Thanksgiving, and that's two months away."

Sean shrugged. "Bailey called Mom last night and the next thing I knew, her and Dad were going to leave first thing this morning to drive up here. They'll arrive in time for our family supper tomorrow night."

"Uh-oh. I wonder which room Mom and Bailey are going to redecorate for you this time?" Blane asked, chuckling.

Sean took a swig of his coffee. "I don't have a clue, but I'm betting Dad will be more than happy to help us out with guard duty. Otherwise, he'll be stuck in the house helping hang pictures or curtains or whatever else they decide they want him to do."

"Yeah, and we all know he'd rather eat a big, ugly bug than to paint or hang wallpaper," Levi added. "Although, I can't say I blame him."

As Carrie listened to the men discuss their parents' upcoming visit and make plans to keep her safe, she decided it might not be all that bad having a plethora of bodyguards. At first, she'd been just a bit insulted by the idea of someone looking out for her when she was perfectly capable of taking care of herself. But the way this man had been coming after her time and time again, she had to admit that she couldn't do this alone. Besides, while they stationed themselves around the ranch, watching for the perp to make his next move, she could start her investigation by searching social media sites for recent activities by some of the poachers she'd arrested. The one thing that poachers couldn't seem to get through their thick skulls was the fact that if they were going to break the law and hunt animals out of season or show off about doing something illegal, they should not, for any reason, brag about what they'd done or were planning to do on their various accounts. It was a surefire way to get caught and one that the WGFD and all law enforcement agencies had capitalized on many times in the past. If this guy was connected to one of the men she'd arrested over a year ago and he'd been dumb enough to outline his plans on social media, it might be the break in the case she needed to end this madness once and for all.

Thad's brothers left to make arrangements with their ranch hands and the Eagle Fork Fire Department to take some time off, while Carrie stayed with him. Once they were gone, he asked, "Would you like to take a tour of the rehab center this afternoon?"

He swallowed hard when she closed her

laptop and worried her lower lip for a moment, as if trying to decide. At that moment, nothing would have pleased him more than to take her in his arms and kiss her, to find out if her lips were as soft as they looked. It took him a moment to realize she'd asked him a question and he berated himself for losing his focus and allowing his mind to wander where it had no business going. "I'm sorry," he said, feeling the all too familiar heat begin to creep up his neck from beneath his collar. "What was that?"

"I asked if you're going to the center now?"

Shaking his head, he explained, "Since we're getting a later start than what I usually do, I thought we could have lunch and then go up there this afternoon. I usually spend Saturdays checking the animals and changing their treatment plans if needed, as well as evaluating the likelihood they'll be able to survive in the wild or if we'll have to find a sanctuary or zoo where they can safely live out the rest of their lives."

"I would love to see your operation," she said, rising from the desk chair. "I'll go make us a couple of sandwiches and pour a couple of glasses of iced tea."

"Sounds good," he said, smiling. "I'll text

Sean and tell him we'll be going up to the center this afternoon and see if he wants to come here to the house or meet us up there."

A couple of hours later, he walked through the kitchen and stepped out the back door to spot Sean walking toward him from the stable. "Where's Carrie?" Sean asked.

"She's getting her vest." He pointed toward the woods behind the stable as he leaned his shoulder against the porch support post and crossed his arms over his chest.

His brother nodded. "You taking the truck?"

"Yup." Under normal circumstances they'd walk, but… "It seemed like the safer option, after what's been going on the past couple of days."

"I agree, little brother." Sean hooked his thumb over his shoulder. "You and Carrie should be all right getting to the truck. It's parked close to the house, and I'll cover her until you both get in, then I'll hop in the back seat and ride up there with you."

Thad nodded. "I talked to Henry earlier and he's aware of what's going on," he said, referring to Henry Black Bear, his assistant manager. "He said he'd stay with our volunteers until they leave for home this evening, just in case. I told him to tell them that the center would be closed for a while so we can inspect enclosures and make needed repairs. They aren't to come back until we call them."

"Good idea." His brother nodded. "Most of your volunteers are high school students, aren't they?"

"Yeah, and I don't want adults getting hurt, let alone a bunch of kids."

When he heard the door behind him open, he turned to find Carrie with a big smile and a twinkle of excitement in her sky blue eyes. "I'm ready when you are," she said, her voice filled with anticipation. "I've been wanting to see the Cougar Mountain Rehabilitation Center since Lyle Markham told me about it when I first arrived in Eagle Fork."

His heart sped up, and he couldn't have stopped his ear to ear grin if his life depended on it. Her enthusiasm for his wildlife rehab operation meant more to him than it probably should, but he wasn't going to question why it filled him with joy. He was just relieved she wasn't turning up her nose like Missy had done at the idea of being around the wildlife. He shook his head as he placed his hand to the small of her back and guided her over to his truck. He needed to stop comparing every woman's reactions with Missy

Franklin's. Carrie was a WGFD warden and it would be highly unlikely she'd be turned off by any animal. *Get a grip, Hanson! Her opinion shouldn't mean any more to you than anyone else's.*

But as he helped her into his truck and waited for Sean to get into the back seat, he couldn't stop grinning, and he knew beyond a shadow of doubt that Carrie's opinion did mean more than anyone else's. In fact, it meant a lot more. What he couldn't seem to get a handle on, was why.

EIGHT

When Thad parked his truck in an open area between a woven wire fence and a collection of different-sized buildings, an older, bandy-legged cowboy was waiting for them. He wore a friendly smile as he limped over to the passenger side window. "Hi, there!" He opened the door and held out his hand to help her down from the truck. "Welcome to the Cougar Mountain Wildlife Rehabilitation Center."

"Thank you," Carrie said, taking his hand to exit the truck. "I'm Game Warden Carrie Caldwell, from the Eagle Fork area office."

"Right—we spoke on the phone the other day. I'm Henry Black Bear. It sure is nice to finally meet you in person, Miss Carrie."

Smiling back at him, she nodded. "And it's very nice to finally meet you, Mr. Black Bear."

"It's just Henry, ma'am," he said, grinning.

"All right… Henry." While Thad and Sean stood by the side of the truck talking in low voices, she assumed about security she'd been told had been set up surrounding the compound, she smiled and got acquainted with the nice old gentleman. "Thad tells me you're his right-hand man here at the center. I'm sorry it took me so long to get out here to see the operation."

The old man nodded. "I'm the manager and head raptor wrangler," he said, laughing. "And it's understandable that you haven't had time to get up here to see us. I heard tell that each WGFD warden has about fifteen hundred square miles they have to watch over. That's a mighty big territory for one person to keep up with."

"There are times it does keep us extremely busy." Staring at him, she couldn't help but like the old man and anticipated a very good working relationship with him and Thad. "If you don't mind me asking, where do you house the animals you're rehabbing?" she asked, looking around.

He pointed to the woven wire fence, and on closer inspection she could see the fence was actually several open-air pens holding mule deer, antelope and a moose calf. A couple of teenagers—probably volunteers—pushing wheelbarrows with hay and buckets full of corn and oats, passed her and Henry to disappear into the woods behind the pens, while a large black, white and tan Bernese mountain dog lumbered over and sat down at her feet. Nudging his big head under her hand, he gazed up at her with adoring eyes.

"That's Max," Henry said, grinning. "He never meets a stranger, and we're pretty sure he thinks everyone comes here just to see him."

"Max, you're a beautiful boy, and I'm more than happy to show you the same adoration you seem to be showing me," Carrie said, kneeling down to scratch behind his ears. Laying his head on top of her knee, the dog closed his eyes and looked as if he was smiling as he clearly enjoyed her attention. Turning to Henry, she asked, "I couldn't figure out where the rehab compound was until Thad drove around the stable and I noticed a little lane going up through the grove of spruce trees behind it."

Henry nodded. "With trucks pulling horse and stock trailers in and out down at the stable and people milling around like a herd of harebrained antelope, there's too much going on for an animal to settle down and be at ease enough to heal. Up here, they have the peace and quiet they need."

"That makes a lot of sense," she said, thinking about some of the wildlife rehab operations she'd seen in other parts of the state. They hadn't paid nearly as much attention to addressing the animals' stress levels as Thad and Henry had.

When Sean walked toward the closest building, Thad joined her and Henry. "I see Max has claimed you as his new best friend."

Hugging the large dog's neck, she rose to her feet. "I'll be his best friend anytime he wants me to be," Carrie said, meaning it.

"Thad, I'm afraid you're gonna have to be the one to give Miss Carrie the grand tour. My arthritis is painin' me somethin' awful. I'm gonna have to sit this one out." Henry reached down and rubbed his knee. "I'll be a mangy-tailed coyote if it ain't rainin' again by mornin'." When he straightened, he took one of Carrie's hands in both of his. "Don't you be a stranger around here, you hear? Drop by anytime." Without another word, he let go of her hand. She watched him limp over to enter a building with a sign that read Raptors before she turned her attention to Thad.

When he smiled at her, she was again reminded of how handsome he was. She had to avert her gaze to the moose calf in the pen across from them to keep from staring at him. Why did she get butterflies in her stomach every time he smiled at her? And why did their wing-flapping acrobatics send awareness coursing through her at the speed of light?

Max nudged her hand again, letting her know that he wanted more attention. "I think you'd be happy if I stood here all day, scratching behind your ears," she said, laughing.

Thad grinned. "He's our official greeter and has the run of my part of the ranch. When he's not hanging out up here at the rehab compound, he's down at the barn, laying in front of the fireplace down at the house or stretched out across my feet while I'm watching television or reading."

"Well, he's one of the sweetest, most amiable dogs I think I've had the pleasure of meeting," she said sincerely, bending down to hug the big fluffy dog again.

"I agree." From the loving expression on his face when he looked at Max, she could tell Thad was as devoted to the dog as the dog was to him. A warm feeling spread throughout her chest and her respect for Thad Hanson rose even further.

Suddenly uncomfortable with how rapidly her admiration for this remarkable man was growing, she looked around for something else to hold her attention, and her gaze landed on a large structure at least a hundred yards from the rest of the buildings and pens. She focused on it as she tried to regain her equilibrium. "Is that where you keep the predators?"

He nodded. "Our goal is to get the sick and injured rehabbed and back out into the wild as soon as possible. That won't happen if we put antelope or deer in a pen near a mountain lion enclosure. They would constantly be catching each other's scent and fear and agitation aren't conducive to healing." He shrugged as he turned toward the nearby pens with deer, and the moose calf. "That's why we have the prey animals as far away from the predators as possible and, since the wind usually blows from the west, we put the pens to the south and the predator enclosures to the north."

"It sounds like you've thought of everything." She walked over to the fence where the moose calf was held. She noted approvingly that he immediately ran to the opposite side of the pen. That was as it should be—wild animals shouldn't feel too comfortable with or dependent on humans. Not if they were going to have to survive in the wild again later on. "How are you managing to maintain the animals' natural wariness?"

"No one is allowed to interact with the animals unless they're feeding them, cleaning the pens or helping me administer medical treatment." He pointed toward the calf as he and Max walked beside her. "See the gate over there behind him?"

"I do now." Until they walked up to the fence, the opposite side of the pen blended in with the forest foliage.

"These are actually holding pens connected to the enclosures just inside the woods beyond. When the volunteers get ready to clean them, they open the gates to let the animals into these pens. After they finish cleaning, they put out fresh hay, grain or whatever is included in the animals' diets, as well as refill water troughs." He returned her smile of understanding. "Then they open the gates, the animals return to their enclosures in the woods and there's minimal interaction with humans."

"And having the pens in the woods is more natural than out in the open," she said, nodding.

"That's the idea. We're keeping them largely in their own natural habitat, as well as reducing their exposure to humans." He rocked back on his heels. "So now that you've seen how we handle the prey animals, do you have any suggestions for improvements?"

"No. From what I've seen you've done an excellent job. It's above and beyond anything I've seen at any other rehabilitation facility." His thoughtful planning was extremely impressive. They started toward the building housing the predator enclosures.

"Josie, could you and Evie take Max into the office?" Thad asked when two teenage girls walked past them toward the buildings. "We're getting ready to go into the predator barn, and I don't want him or the bobcats getting agitated."

"Sure," the one he'd called Josie said, smiling. "Come on, Maxie, let's go see what Mr. Henry needs us to do before we go home."

"Would it be okay to give him a treat, Dr. Thad?" the younger girl asked hopefully.

"As long as it's only one, Evie." Thad grinned as he placed his hand to Carrie's back and guided her toward the predator barn. "Max is gaining a little more weight than he should."

As the girls nodded and led the dog to the main office, Carrie walked up the hill beside him. "How do you go about releasing animals when they've been successfully rehabbed?" she asked. "Do you try to release the animals in the area where they were found?"

"We do." He opened the door to the building and held it for her to enter ahead of him. "In a few days, the team and I will be releasing a couple of bobcats. Would you like to go with us?"

Without having to think twice, she nodded. "Absolutely."

His pleased smile made her knees feel a little weak as he motioned toward what looked like oversize dog runs with two juvenile-looking bobcats. "These are the only predators we have right now." He stopped in front of the runs. "These two are brothers, Art and Bart. They were about six months old and severely malnourished when they and their sister were found abandoned on Sean's part of the ranch. The female didn't make it, and we weren't sure these two would pull through. But they did, and now they're ready to take their place on the mountain."

The pride in his voice attested to his love for animals and for the job he was obviously born to do. While he watched the bobcats, she realized he was assessing their condition and readiness to be released. She found herself feeling a bit envious. Although she loved what she did, protecting wildlife and stopping those who tried to hunt out of season, she would really rather be more hands-on with the animals and if possible, care for and rehab some of them the way Thad and Henry were doing.

When Thad's phone rang, he excused himself and walked several feet away to take the call. While he talked with someone about an injured horse, Carrie observed the behavior of the bobcats. They were quickly reaching the age where they would part ways to live, as was inherent to their species. An adult, male bobcat maintained a solitary life, avoiding other males and only interacting with female bobcats during the mating season.

"I'm sorry, but we're going to have to cut the tour short," he apologized. "I have an emergency ranch call I have to go to."

"Do you mind if I tag along?" she asked as they left the predator building and walked across the compound toward his truck. She'd love to see him in action, doing the job he was so passionate about.

Grinning, he shook his head. "I don't mind at all. You can be my assistant. You don't have a problem with the sight of blood, do you?"

"Only if it's mine," she said honestly. She wasn't going to mention that she hadn't been overly sensitive even about the sight of her own blood until she'd become involved with Chip Wilford. Whenever he became enraged over something she'd said or done, she had always ended up with a scrape, cuts or at the very least a bloody nose. She'd come to associate the sight of her own blood with pain, discomfort and gut-wrenching fear.

When they reached the truck, Sean was waiting for them. After Thad helped her into the truck, they both got in. "I've got a ranch call I have to go to," he explained to his brother. "One of John Armstrong's mares has a deep gash on her shoulder that needs stitches."

"What happened to the mare?" Sean asked.

"You know how horses are." Thad shrugged as he steered the truck down the lane leading to the ranch yard. "You can wrap them in bubble wrap, put them in a padded stall and they'll still find a way to hurt themselves."

"I've heard my dad say something similar every time he has to call the vet to patch up one of his ranch horses," Carrie said, laughing.

When Thad stopped his truck next to his brother's, Sean got out and, just before he closed the door, warned, "Watch your six and call if you need us. I'll follow you to the Rocking A, then head back to my part of the ranch. Levi and Blane will be waiting for you at the end of Armstrong's ranch road to follow you home."

"Do you think it's safe to go on this call?" she asked as they started down the lane to the main road. Given the trouble they'd had for the past few days, she felt the question needed to be asked.

"I hope so." He shook his head. "I can't let an animal suffer, and since I'm the only vet in this county, I have to go and see what I can do for her. The Rocking A is only a couple of miles down the road from my part of the ranch, and we shouldn't have any problems with Sean following us." He gave her a smile as the lights of Sean's truck illuminated the inside of his truck. "And Levi and Blane will be over soon, too. They'll follow us back to my place."

As he drove his truck down the long, winding drive that would eventually intersect with the main road, Carrie tried to relax and enjoy the trip—but she couldn't stop herself from glancing around every few seconds, making sure the attacker wasn't about to strike. She hated that her tormentor had made her fearful all over again. When Chip had been sent to prison, much of the fear she'd had for her life had disappeared. And once she'd learned that he'd died behind bars, she had relaxed even further. She hadn't wanted to hear of his death, but there had been such relief in knowing for certain the threat he had posed would never plague her again.

But now here she was. In danger again and, this time it was worse.

At least when Chip had threatened her, she knew why he was doing it, could visibly see who wanted her to die. But now she had no idea why the Drone Jerk would feel that the world would be a better place without her. Who could possibly hold so much hatred in their hearts that they would go to extraordinary lengths to end her life?

* * *

"Easy, babe." Thad's voice was low and soothing as he stroked the palomino mare's golden coat. "What did you run into? I have a feeling whatever it was, it came out of the encounter better than you did."

His calm voice and gentle manner were mesmerizing. Carrie was awed by his way with the animal. When they arrived, the horse had been agitated, repeatedly shying away from being touched, but the moment Thad started talking to her, gently running his hands over her silky hide, the mare settled noticeably and stood quietly while he assessed the large, deep tear on her shoulder.

"Do you think you can patch her up without leaving too much of a scar, Doc?" the owner asked.

On the way to his neighbor's ranch, Thad had told her that John Armstrong raised champion pleasure horses and entered them in horse shows all over the country. Carrie knew enough about show horses to know that, although a judge wasn't supposed to score a horse lower because of scarring, judges did have their preferences when it came to appearance. An unsightly mark could influence them into giving the animal a lower score.

"I can't make any guarantees, John," Thad answered without taking his attention from the mare. "This is deep and it's really ragged. But I'm going to trim it up and do my best to keep the scar as neat and unnoticeable as I can. The rest will be up to you to keep it clean and dressed, as well as be on the lookout for any signs of infection until the sutures are removed."

The man nodded. "That's all I can ask, Doc. You know I take great pains to make sure my horses are well cared for."

A couple of hours later, when she and Thad walked out of the barn into the darkness of evening, Carrie realized that she was truly in awe of him. His skill and care in treating the horse were truly incredible. He'd given the mare an injection of a mild sedative and a local pain block to numb the area, but it was his kind, soothing words as he worked to close the shoulder wound that she was certain calmed the horse more than the drugs. He continually reassured the mare in that calming voice he'd used from the moment he approached her, and the animal stood completely still the entire time he worked to suture the gash closed. When he finished and administered an injection of antibiotics, he placed his palm on the mare's neck and, bowing his head, said a quiet prayer for her to heal quickly with little pain and minimal scarring.

"You're a wonderful veterinarian," Carrie said, feeling compelled to let him know. "I've seen a lot of vets over the years when my father called them to our ranch, but I've never seen anyone who showed the level of compassion and caring that you used with that mare, nor have I ever seen one send up prayers for an animal."

"I've always loved animals," he said, helping her into his truck. After he walked around the front to slide in behind the steering wheel, he added, "And I find they calm down and accept what I have to do for them a lot easier when I continually talk to them. And praying for the animals I treat comes as natural as breathing."

"Well, what you're doing works and I fully understand why Blane calls you Dolittle," she said, smiling. "He was a wonderful veterinarian who had a special ability to communicate with the animals, just like you do in your own way."

He smiled and shook his head, reaching over to cover her hand with his. "While I appreciate your faith in my abilities, I'm just doing what I was trained to do. I'm sure any other vet would do just as well."

As they drove up the lane from the Rocking A ranch toward the main highway, Thad continued to hold her hand and she didn't even think to pull away from his touch. She was too busy marveling at the man he'd shown himself to be. She could tell from the genuine tone of his voice that he really didn't feel he'd done anything extraordinary. But she knew better. This cowboy veterinarian with a heart of gold had talked to the mare and calmed her down, using the same calming voice and gentle touch that he'd used to reassure her when he'd picked her up and carried her away from the WGFD truck. His manner and tranquil tone instilled trust and acceptance, and whether he realized it or not, it was a rare quality.

She valued it even more when she realized how humble he was, seeming genuinely surprised that anyone would consider him worthy of recognition for his gifts. When she had been in a relationship with Chip, he had expected praise and admiration ad nauseam for anything and everything. But Thad had downplayed the importance of his role in the successful outcome of treating the horse, and she found his humility to not only be refreshing, but endearing. She just kept finding new things to like about the man.

Her heart stalled and she shook her head to dislodge the thought. She had no business finding any man refreshing, endearing, likeable or anything else. There was a very good reason she'd avoided having a relationship with another man after her ex-boyfriend. With him she'd been naive and therefore trusted that he cared for her as much as she cared for him. It wasn't until he'd beat her a few times that she'd realized how wrong she'd been about him. But by then, he'd gotten her so twisted around that she hadn't known how to extract herself from the relationship. He'd eroded her confidence to the point where she felt like she couldn't handle being without him—and then he'd tried to control every aspect of her life.

It wasn't until his attacks turned deadly that she'd stopped lying to herself. In the aftermath of the trial, she had come to the conclusion that she had very poor judgment when it came to men and she was better off without one.

Deciding it was time to get her mind off the past, when they reached the main road, she asked, "Weren't Levi and Blane supposed to meet us here?"

Thad nodded. "Here comes a set of headlights. That has to be them now." He steered his truck onto the highway and headed toward his entrance to the Cougar Mountain Ranch.

Seconds later, she knew something was wrong when the truck began to accelerate.

"Carrie, make sure your seat belt is tight and hold on," Thad said, suddenly interrupting her thoughts as he released her hand to grip the steering wheel with both of his. His voice had become tight, and he kept glancing into the rearview mirror as he increased the truck's speed. "That's not my brother. That vehicle is coming up too fast. I think our attacker is back."

When the lights of the truck behind them were so close they disappeared behind the tailgate of his truck, Thad increased his speed again in hopes of lessening the effects of the crash he was sure was inevitable and braced for the impact he knew was coming. The brush guard on the sinister black vehicle caused a deafening screech as metal met metal. The jarring thud caused his seat belt harness to bite into his shoulder. Fortunately his truck was big enough and heavy enough that he was able to retain control. That helped, but wasn't a guarantee that they wouldn't end up running off the road or in a serious accident.

"Your driveway is coming up, isn't it?" Carrie asked, her voice shaky and higher than normal from the fear he knew she was experiencing.

"Yeah, but we're going too fast to make the turn," he answered. If they could make it another couple of miles without crashing, the terrain flattened out into a valley between Cougar Mountain and Tranquility Peak. That would lessen the chance of running off into a ravine, or worse yet, running off into the small river that ran parallel to the road. It wasn't a particularly deep or even wide tributary, but it was swift and could easily carry a vehicle downstream to the waterfall where the river fell to the valley below.

Nodding at his phone in the tray on the center console, he continued to race toward the nearest level stretch of road. "Carrie, call Levi and let him and Blane know what's going on," Thad said, pressing the gas pedal all the way to the floor. When his truck surged forward, a space between the two vehicles opened up.

"Tell him we're headed down the highway toward the valley between his driveway and mine." Now, if they could just make it to that point, they'd have a better chance of surviving this insanity.

As Carrie made the call, they reached the valley and the black truck closed the distance between them, once again ramming his tailgate. The violent jolt caused the back of his dually to fishtail, but he managed to maintain control. Looking in his rearview mirror, he groaned when he saw the angle the other driver was taking. Instead of coming at them to hit the tailgate dead center as he'd done before, the jerk was going to ram them on the right back corner of the truck bed. The impact had a good chance of sending them into a spin or causing the truck to roll.

"Hold on!" he shouted, trying to warn Carrie.

He'd no sooner gotten the words out than the smaller truck hit his dually full force. Thad felt the right back wheels lift off the pavement, the momentum sending the vehicle into a deadly roll. With no way to stop what was happening, he instinctively reached out for Carrie. Finding her hand, he held on as their shoulder harnesses held them in place while the truck continued to turn over and over. A sharp pain at the back of his head, followed by a shower of glass, caused his vision to narrow as a dark tunnel began to close in around him. He struggled to part the shadows, to stay conscious long enough to see that Carrie was all right and protected from their assailant, but the pull of the darkness was more than he could fight. His last thought as he quietly slipped into the peace of the dark abyss was to ask God to please keep her safe in His care.

NINE

When Thad's truck stopped its violent roll, Carrie was amazed to realize that it had landed upright in the field beside the road. Mentally doing a physical self-check, she ascertained that she could move her arms and legs without pain. Although she had a few minor cuts that were stinging a bit and her shoulder was sore from the seat belt strap, she didn't seem to be hurt.

"Thad, are you…all right?" she asked. When he remained silent, she turned her head to look at him. "Please tell me you're okay." It was dark and extremely hard to see without the lights from the dashboard, but she could tell that his head was hanging with his chin resting on his chest, and he wasn't moving or responding to her.

"Dear Lord, please let him be okay. Please."

Her hands shook as she fumbled to release her seat belt and reach over to place her index and middle finger along the side of his neck. Thankfully, his pulse was strong and steady—but when she drew her hand back, something sticky coated her fingers. She instinctively knew it was blood. He obviously had a head wound and had been knocked out at some point during the crash.

Suddenly the truck cab was filled with a blinding light, and when she heard the revving of an engine, she knew it was the black truck. The driver seemed to have positioned the vehicle so the headlights illuminated the wreckage. He was probably assessing whether they were alive or dead so he could determine what his next move would be. *God, please send help. Please let Thad's brothers arrive in time to keep things from getting worse.*

The driver continued revving the engine of the sinister black truck. He was probably increasing the rpm of the motor in order to gain additional speed when he took his foot off the brake to slam into them again.

Her heart pounded hard against her rib cage when the truck came a little closer, then stopped to rev the engine again. He was taunting them, heightening the suspense before he finished them off. Pulling her gun from the holster on her belt, she prepared to protect Thad, as well as defend herself. Just when she thought the truck lights would surely blind her, the black truck's engine growled as the driver shifted gears as it spun around, drove back onto the road and raced away in the opposite direction.

For a few beats, Carrie could only sit there, blinking in disbelief. It didn't seem possible that whoever was in the driver's seat had decided to give up terrorizing them and was heading back the way he'd come from. It took a moment for her to grasp that there was a big dual-wheel truck coming down the road from the opposite direction at a high rate of speed. When it came to a sliding halt on the blacktop road thirty feet from where Thad's truck had come to rest, she watched two men jump out and run across the expanse toward them. She prayed they were Thad's brothers.

"Are you and Thad all right?" Blane asked, sticking his head through the open passenger window where the glass had shattered during the rollover.

"Thad's...h-hurt," she said, fighting to keep her emotions under control. "P-please do...something." When the driver's door was forced open by a mighty tug, she realized that Levi had gone around the truck and was tearing down the curtain airbag to get to Thad.

"Blane, call 9-1-1. Tell them to send an ambulance. Then get in touch with Sean and tell him to get here ASAP," Levi ordered. Glancing at her, he asked, "Was Thad knocked out during the crash or did he lose consciousness after?"

"I think he was knocked out when the truck rolled," she answered. "His head is bleeding on the right side somewhere behind his ear."

Levi nodded as he gently examined his brother's head and shoulders. "Was the truck we saw speeding away from here the one that caused this?"

She nodded. "He hit the back of Thad's truck and caused us to roll."

"Did you get a license plate number or see who was driving?" he continued questioning her.

"I'm sorry, no. Everything happened so fast and it was dark," she answered, feeling like she had failed. As a peace officer she should have been more observant of the details.

When Blane finished making the calls, he opened the passenger door and turned his attention to her. "Do you think anything is broken, Carrie? Are you in pain? And if so, where?"

"No, I have a few minor cuts from broken glass, but that's all," she said, unable to take her eyes off Thad. "I'm fine, really. Please just take care of Thad." As she watched, she thought she saw his head lift a fraction of an inch. She wondered if she'd imagined it— but then a moment later, he slowly raised it from his chest.

Thank You, Lord, she prayed silently as she exhaled a sigh of relief.

"Easy, little brother," Levi warned. "I need to get a cervical collar on you before you move around too much."

"I'm…okay. Make s-sure… Carrie ish… all right," he said, his words hesitant and a bit slurred.

"I'm all right, Thad." Her gaze flew to Levi's, silently asking what was wrong.

"Thad, I'm pretty sure you have a concussion," Levi answered, nodding as his eyes met hers. He drew a cervical collar from his paramedic's bag to position it around Thad's neck. "We'll know for sure after a CT scan and X-rays."

She could tell Thad wasn't happy about having the restrictive brace around his neck.

Taking hold of his hand to keep him from reaching up to release it, she glanced at Levi. The man's face reflected his stubborn determination to keep the collar in place, no matter how his younger brother felt about it. While he worked on placing a bandage over the laceration on Thad's head, she gave Thad what she hoped was an encouraging smile. "I think it's only a precaution at the moment, and you might not have to wear it after you're checked out at the hospital." Several minutes later, the sound of sirens in the distance was reassuring. She hoped they hurried because Thad was looking extremely frustrated. "Please, Thad, it's to protect you from further injury. I'm sure your brother would feel better if you wear it until a doctor has a chance to look at you. And I know I will."

"Are you…all right?" he asked, his eyes looking more focused as he searched her face.

She nodded. "I'm fine, and I'm sure I can get someone to give me a ride to the hospital if I start feeling like I need to seek medical attention."

Levi cleared his throat. "About that. You do realize I'm going to advise you to be checked out at the hospital, as well, don't you?"

Before she could protest, Thad squeezed

her hand. "If I have to go, you do, too. You can even ride in the ambulance with me," he said, giving her that smile that never failed to release butterflies in her stomach.

"I doubt they would allow me to do that. EMS usually doesn't want more than one patient in an ambulance at a time." She was confident that Levi would back her up on that. But when she looked at him, he grinned and she knew before he opened his mouth that she would be riding to the hospital with Thad.

"No problem. If that's what it takes to get you both to be checked out properly, I can make that happen."

It was three in the morning before Thad was given the go-ahead to remove the aggravating collar. The ER docs had reluctantly conceded that his neck and spine appeared to be uninjured, though he was advised to take it easy until he went for a recheck with his doctor at the end of the upcoming week. The CT scan had confirmed that he did have a mild concussion. The doctor had wanted him to stay in the hospital for the rest of the night for observation, but eventually gave his approval and told Thad he could go home as long as he got plenty of rest. Thad was certain it was only due to the fact that the doctor knew the head of Eagle Fork's EMS team would be staying with him for the next few days that he relented.

"Where's Carrie?" he asked as Blane stepped around the curtain to his hospital bed. He'd pulled on his clothes as soon as the doctor had assured him his discharge papers would be ready within fifteen minutes and he'd be free to go. That had been thirty minutes ago and he was done waiting on them. He was going home whether the papers were ready or not.

"She's sitting in the waiting area with Levi and Sean." His brother grinned. "They're telling her all about the boneheaded things you did when you were a little kid and how many times you ended up at the ER to get stitches."

He groaned. "That's just peachy. Now she probably thinks I'm the biggest klutz to ever walk on two legs. And I don't suppose you told her that half of the times I needed to be sewn up was because one of the three of you put me up to doing something stupid."

Blane eyed him for a few seconds before his mouth split into a wide grin. "So her opinion of you matters that much, huh?"

"Knock it off, Blane." He moved to stand up and his brother was at his side in a heartbeat.

"Whoa, little brother, slow down. It's hospital policy that you take a ride to the doors in a wheelchair."

"I don't need a wheelchair," he said, gritting his teeth to keep from losing his temper. "And I don't need my brothers telling anyone what a screwup I've always been. I've already managed to prove that to her several times." He rarely ever got riled about much of anything, but at the moment, Blane's snarky grin and the idea of his brothers telling Carrie tales about his clumsiness around girls were really pushing his buttons. Never mind the insistence that he had to ride in the wheelchair, making him look weak and pathetic in front of her. "I'm perfectly capable of walking out of here on my own steam, and that's exactly what I'm going to do."

His brother fell into step beside him as he walked out into the hall and headed toward the ER nurses station. "I'm leaving now," Thad told the nurse behind the desk. "Are my discharge papers ready or would you like to mail them to me?"

"I'm sorry for the delay, Dr. Hanson," the nurse said, handing him the physician's instructions. "I was just getting ready to bring them to you."

He nodded. "Thanks."

"Wait," she said, jumping to her feet to come around the desk when he turned to leave. "I'll get a wheelchair."

"I prefer to walk," Thad said, heading toward the swinging doors rather than sticking around to argue. Years of listening to his mother cautioning him to mind his manners and never to be rude had him adding, "But thanks for the offer."

"But…"

"I'll see that he gets to the truck without a problem," Blane assured the woman as he stuck close to him.

As he and Blane walked through the swinging double doors into the waiting room, Thad's gaze went immediately to Carrie. Now that his head was a little clearer, he needed to make sure she really was all right. There were a couple of small bandages on her forehead and along her jaw and a larger one on her hand, but otherwise she appeared to have fared better in the wreck than he had. He was grateful for that.

"How are you feeling?" she asked, rising from her chair to face him. "Did you have to have stitches or staples to close the laceration on your head?"

"Yeah, the doctor told me it took five staples—and the lousy haircut was on the house," he said, running his hand over the short stubble where his hair had been before the doctor clipped it back to treat the deep cut.

She smiled and raised her hand as if to touch his head, but then dropped it back down to her side. "Your hair will grow back, and it doesn't look as bad as you think," she said softly, her voice turning his insides to mush.

He would have liked nothing more than to take her in his arms and hold her, to breathe her in and feel her warmth to affirm that she was really unharmed, but all three of his brothers were way more interested in what was going on between them than they were in bringing the truck to the ER entrance for the ride home. Besides, she hadn't shown the slightest interest in anything more than friendship where he was concerned.

"Who drove?" he finally asked.

"Blane drove my truck while I rode with you two in the ambulance," Levi answered. He held his hand out to Blane for his key fob, then walked out to the parking lot to get his truck.

"I'm heading back to my place," Sean announced. "Bailey is a little under the weather and I need to get back. Besides, I don't like leaving her with this idiot on the loose."

"You didn't leave her alone tonight, did you?" Thad asked, feeling more guilty by the minute. If anything happened to the young woman they all loved like a sister, he'd never forgive himself.

Sean shook his head. "I have a couple of my men standing guard at both entrance doors to the house."

"Good," Thad and Blane said at the same time.

"Thanks for showing up in time to keep things from going from bad to worse," Thad said, giving each of his brothers a one-arm hug. His family was the best and he thanked God every day that he had their love and support.

"You know we always have your back no matter what," Sean said.

"The same as you have ours," Blane added.

Without thinking, Thad took Carrie's hand in his as they all walked in silence toward the ER exit. When they stepped out into the crisp, early morning air, he looked up at the vast array of stars still twinkling above. The sight never failed to humble him, as well as remind him of God's infinite love and grace.

"Thank you, Lord, for keeping Carrie and me safe from those who seek to harm us," he whispered. A chorus of amens from his brothers and the woman at his side surrounded him.

When Levi stopped the truck, Sean helped Thad into the front passenger seat. Blane helped Carrie into the back seat of the vehicle and closed the door. "Levi and I will be staying with you until he has to go back to work at the firehouse next week," Blane said, his expression as serious as Thad had ever seen on his brother's face.

"We've also decided to have our Sunday night supper over at your place tonight," Sean said. "That way you and Carrie can still be with us while you both follow the doctor's orders and take it easy. And I've asked the DCI investigator to wait until later this morning to take your statements. I figured it would help to have some rest before you answer all the questions."

"Are you sure having everyone over at my place is a good idea? What about the danger?" Thad asked. "Mom and Bailey..."

Blane laughed. "You know Mom's every bit as good of a shot as any one of us."

"And I've been working with Bailey," Sean

added. "She's more comfortable with firearms now and doesn't have any problem hitting what she's aiming at." He shook his head. "I seriously doubt this jerk is going to want to take on the fight that a Hanson family gathering could produce. Every one of us are going to be ready and willing to defend ourselves and the family. He'd be an idiot not to figure out what that means in terms of *his* safety."

Blane grinned. "Yeah, and if he'd wanted to take that kind of chance, he would have hung around in the valley instead of tucking his tail and running like a scared rabbit when Levi and I showed up."

Emotion clogged Thad's throat, making it impossible to speak. When a Hanson was threatened, whoever had the guts—or more accurately, the stupidity—to take on the one had better be prepared to stand against the entire bunch, because that was exactly what he was going to get. He felt blessed beyond words.

"Ready to go?" Levi asked, putting his big dually in gear when Sean closed the passenger door and started across the parking lot to his truck, while Blane climbed into the back seat next to Carrie.

Thad nodded as he buckled his seat belt.

"Yeah, I'm more than ready to get back to Cougar Mountain where we all belong."

The evening after the accident, Carrie stood out of the way in the pantry doorway as Thad's family filed into his kitchen, their arms loaded down with containers and slow cookers full of food. Of course, she'd got to know his brothers already, but this was the first time she'd be meeting his parents and Sean's wife, Bailey. Normally, she wasn't overly nervous or hesitant around new people, but this was Thad's family and she couldn't help but wonder if they held her responsible for what had happened last night. She honestly wouldn't blame them if they did. She certainly felt guilty about it. If it weren't for her, the accident most likely wouldn't have happened and Thad wouldn't be recovering from a concussion.

"You must be Carrie," a petite woman with beautiful long coppery-red hair said as she walked over to hug her. "I'm Bailey Hanson, Sean's wife." She paused for a moment, then a big smile lit her pretty face as she confided, "I just love saying that."

"It's really nice to meet you, Bailey," Carrie said, immediately liking the woman. About the same age as herself, Carrie could tell right away that Bailey Hanson was one of those people who was outgoing, kind and affectionate—as pretty on the inside as she was on the outside. "And congratulations on your recent marriage."

"Thank you, but we actually got married a few months ago. Unfortunately, we had to wait to go on our honeymoon because I needed to be available to testify in court." Her smile was filled with sympathy as she took hold of Carrie's hands. "About a year ago, I was in your shoes. I was being chased by a horrible man who wanted nothing more than to kill me. That's how Sean and I met. He was protecting me for the FBI."

"That's terrible," Carrie said. "I'm so glad it all worked out for you and Sean."

The young woman wore a wide grin. "Me, too. I finally got to be part of a big, noisy family like I've always wanted."

"Hi, I'm Ann Hanson, Thad's mother," a woman in her late fifties or early sixties said as she joined them. Tall and willowy, Mrs. Hanson was very attractive and didn't look old enough to be the mother of men the ages of the Hanson brothers. She pointed to the man across the kitchen, talking to the four brothers who were younger versions of him. "That's Mike, my husband." She laughed when he looked up and winked at her from across the room. "I often tell people he's my oldest child." It was easy to see the couple were as in love with each other today as they'd been when they first wed.

Carrie's chest tightened and she took a deep breath to ease the ache of disappointment for things that could never be. She didn't think she'd ever be able to trust a man enough to start dating again, let alone to marry someone and start a family. Her gaze automatically sought out Thad. If there was one man she thought she might be able to trust… *Don't go there.*

"I'm glad to meet both of you," Carrie said, meaning it. "I just wish it was under better circumstances." She felt guilty for bringing so much danger to the Cougar Mountain Ranch and this warm, welcoming family.

Ann put her arm around Carrie's shoulders. "Don't you dare blame yourself for what's been going on, honey. You didn't ask for this and it's not your fault. The blame rests squarely on the shoulders of the man who's threatening you and my son."

"Thank you, Mrs. Hanson, but I'll still feel

better when there's no longer any danger to anyone—especially your family."

"I understand." She put her other arm around Bailey's shoulders and pulled them both into a loving hug. "Now, what do you say we run these men out of here so we can finish getting supper ready and the table set?"

While Mrs. Hanson shooed her husband and sons out, Carrie made a solemn vow to step up her investigation first thing in the morning. She was going to leave no stone unturned in her quest to find out who was behind this trouble so that the danger to the Hanson family could end. Then, once she'd helped to restore peace on the ranch, she'd leave the mountain and request a transfer to another part of the state. Sticking around so close to Thad and his wonderful family was going to cause her to want things that she knew for certain were not in her future.

TEN

The following day, Carrie sat back from Thad's desktop computer, her frustration palpable. Since her laptop had either been taken or destroyed during the ransacking of the WGFD station, he'd offered his computer in order for her to start her investigation. She could tell he preferred the idea of her investigating from behind a computer screen. It was less likely to put her back in harm's way and she was fine with that, as long as it helped close the case. The only problem was, her plan hadn't gone the way she'd hoped.

She'd searched all morning for anything she could find through social media and archived news reports, as well as the state law enforcement databases—but she could find absolutely nothing significant to implicate the group of poachers she'd arrested up north last year. The only one who had been sentenced to time in the state prison was still incarcerated, and his two accomplices had apparently been model citizens with no arrests or complaints since they'd paid their fines and forfeited their guns and hunting licenses. It turned out that only one of them had sons, and his kids were still in grade school—far too young to be the attacker Thad had seen. Whoever her attacker was, it didn't seem like he was connected to the poaching ring.

So now where did she start looking for persons of interest? She'd only arrested a handful of other people in her four-year career as a game warden and their infractions had been minor. Certainly nothing to warrant this type of relentless, determined assault. It was looking more and more like Thad was right. The threat had to have come from her personal life. But who could it be? Chip was the only person she could think of who had ever wanted to hurt her, and he was gone now.

When her phone rang, the interruption was almost a relief. At least the break from her search might bring down the level of her frustration and enable her to think more clearly. Glancing at the caller ID, she cringed. She hadn't told her parents and brothers about the attacks, but they had no doubt been informed by some of their friends in law enforcement.

Taking a deep breath, she swiped the screen to answer the call and put it on speaker. "Hi, Mom."

"Carrie Ann Caldwell, what on earth is going on?" her mother demanded.

She sighed heavily. When her mother started a conversation by using her full, given name it was never a good sign, but it was an indication that she was expected to remain silent and listen unless Beverly Sanderson Caldwell asked a question. "Hello to you, too, Mom." She wasn't about to ask her mother what she meant. She knew. "I'm fine, Mom, and there really isn't anything for you and Dad to be worried about."

"I wasn't born yesterday, young lady. When I'm informed by the head of the DCI that my daughter has been shot at, had her WGFD station destroyed by vandals and been the passenger in a rollover car crash, I know that everything *is not* all right," her mother stated emphatically. "Now, tell me what's going on."

Carrie knew what her mother wanted. She wanted the reason for the attacks and a description of who was responsible. And if she knew that, she'd have put an end to it by now.

But she didn't have a clue, and she knew as surely as she knew her own name, that wasn't going to mollify her mother.

"I'm not entirely sure of anything at this point," Carrie admitted. "I thought the attacks might have been tied to an arrest I made last year, but I've been investigating and that hunch turned out to be a dead end."

"Where are you now? I'll send one of your brothers to get you and bring you home."

"No!" She hadn't intended to be so forceful, but she needed her mother to know that she was staying put. She was a grown woman who made her own decisions and therefore had the right to stay and assist in bringing her assailant to justice. Calming herself, she continued, "I'm going to stay here and help with the investigation. I'm not going to allow whoever is behind this to make me run away. Thanks to Chip, I've let fear rule my life before—and I'm not going to let it happen again. You're the one who's always saying that we can't let fear win. As a prosecutor, you should appreciate my stance on this, Mom."

Her mother was silent for several long moments before a quiet sob preceded her words. "The difference...is that you're my daughter."

"I know you and Dad love me and you're

extremely concerned for my well-being, but I have to do this, Mom," she said, miserable that she was upsetting her mother to the point of shedding tears. Beverly Sanderson Caldwell wasn't a woman who cried easily. In fact, the only other time she'd known of her mother crying was when her parents rushed to the hospital the night Chip had almost killed her.

"Care Bear?" Her mother had apparently put the phone on speaker. When she heard her father's deep voice say the nickname he'd called her for her entire life, it felt like a warm, reassuring hug.

"Hey, Daddy," she said softly. His rich baritone never failed to make her feel secure and so very cherished.

"I just got off the phone with the prosecutor down in Casper who handled the case against Chip Wilford. He told me something I think you need to know."

She sat up straight. "I'm listening."

"DA Bennett said he was contacted by Chip's mother about a week ago, telling him she was afraid one or both of her remaining sons were planning to commit a crime. When he asked why she thought that, she told him she'd found her basement full of guns and ammunition, as well as tactical gear and body armor. He sent a DCI investigator to check it out, and although it was an excessive amount of firepower, everything had been purchased legally and was within the legal limits. There was nothing the law could do. But they were continuing to watch both of them…and they've lost track of the youngest one."

"I can't believe either one of them could be behind this. I've always gotten along great with Chip's family," she said incredulously. "Mrs. Wilford even apologized after Chip was found guilty and told me I'd done the right thing putting an end to his cruelty. And both of his brothers said I would always be the sister they never had."

"The youngest was pretty young when it happened," her father pointed out. "Maybe his perspective changed once he got older. I'm going to consult a couple of PIs I've used in the past and see what they can dig up." He paused for a moment, then asked, "Are you safe where you are, Care Bear?"

"Yes, I am," Carrie stated without hesitation. "I'm staying on the Cougar Mountain Ranch with the Hanson family. They own the mountain. They've been wonderful and opened their homes to me for as long as I need to stay."

"Is one of them named Sean?" her father asked.

"Yes. Do you know him?"

"Not personally, but I've heard nothing but good things about him as a former FBI agent," he answered. "I've also heard he's the best wildlife photographer in the Rockies now."

"The entire family is amazing. They're all civic-minded, involved in helping the Eagle Fork community and strong advocates of conservation and wildlife preservation," she said, trying not to gush. When Thad entered the room and walked over to rest one hip on the corner of the desk, she smiled. "Listen, I need to go, but try not to worry. I'm safe here and hopefully this will end soon. And Dad, please call if you find out anything else."

"Sweetie, we love you," her mother said, sniffing. "Please stay safe and thank the Hanson family for us for watching over you. We'll be praying for all of you."

"I will. I love you both to the moon and back and always have you in my prayers," Carrie said, nodding.

"Love you. Stay safe, Care Bear," her father said gruffly.

"Bye."

When she ended the call, she looked up

into Thad's handsome face. "I suppose you heard. My mother and father want me to thank you and your family for keeping me safe and letting me stay here."

"It's our pleasure." His sincere smile sent the butterflies in her stomach into a fluttering frenzy. The room suddenly felt like oxygen was in short supply. "I didn't mean to eavesdrop, but I heard you tell your dad to give you a call if he learned anything else. Has he uncovered something about what's been going on?"

Carrie took a deep breath as she tried to decide how much of her past, if any, she should share with him. After testifying at the trial, she hadn't really talked about her experience with Chip to anyone other than her parents and her therapist. She'd felt so fragile, so scarred, physically and emotionally, and she had struggled with opening up and potentially allowing others to see her that way, too. But as she stared into Thad's warm brown eyes, she knew for certain she could trust him to keep her secrets and not to think any less of her. He'd proven time after time that he was trustworthy and that he viewed her with both compassion and respect. She hadn't forgotten how naturally he'd handled her claustrophobia when she'd refused to go into the root cellar. But still she hesitated.

It had less to do with trusting him and more to do with her lingering anger at herself. She felt such humiliation and shame about how faulty her judgment had been, how she'd been so wrong about Chip and how long she had overlooked the signs of his true nature. And how she'd allowed him to manipulate her into staying with him after the abuse started. She should have gotten away from him long before everything had a chance to go so wrong, to turn so dangerous.

Did she have the courage to tell Thad how foolish she'd been and how it had almost cost her her life? Was she prepared to risk seeing the concern and compassion in his eyes turn to disbelief and disappointment for the foolish, naive girl she'd once been?

She took a fortifying breath and looked deeply into his kind brown eyes. "I'm not sure where to begin." She closed her eyes and swallowed hard as she decided the beginning was the only place to start. "I met a boy my freshman year at the University of Wyoming. His name was Chip Wilford."

Thad could tell Carrie was struggling with what she was about to say and wondered what could have possibly happened to cause her the amount of anguish he was detecting in her expressive blue eyes. Had she lost the love of her life to a tragic accident? Or had her heart been broken by this guy in her past the way his ex-girlfriend had decimated his?

"What happened?"

"Nothing...at first." She stared past his shoulder, and he could tell she was reaching back into her past for memories that she'd rather not deal with. "He seemed sweet, fun. Kind of possessive, but I didn't mind that—I just thought it meant that he was really into me. But after a few months there were some subtle changes in our relationship. I tried to dismiss them as him just being concerned and a little overly protective."

A sick feeling began to coil in the pit of his belly. "It wasn't protectiveness, was it?"

When she shook her head, the coil tightened. "He started making demands that I give up my dreams of being a WGFD officer and working with wildlife. He said I didn't have to work—that he would take care of me. He didn't seem to understand that I *wanted* to build a career. He took it as an attack on him, as if I was saying that I didn't trust him to be a good provider. Meanwhile, he didn't trust *me* at all. Any time I was out of his sight, he was constantly calling me, checking up on me, making sure I actually was where I said I'd be. He tried to control everything I did, everywhere I went and everyone I associated with. He didn't even want me keeping in close touch with my parents the way I had always done. When I refused to cut ties with them…"

His heart felt like it stopped, and he couldn't seem to draw in his next breath. He figured he knew what had happened, but instead of voicing his speculation about what had taken place, he remained silent, sensing her need to tell him, her need to confront what happened in the past.

She bowed her head, and he watched as first one, then another tear dropped onto her tightly knotted hands resting in her lap. "He started…hitting me." It was clear that it had been difficult to get those words out, but after that, it seemed to come easier, as if voicing what happened had eased something inside of her, released some of the pressure holding her back. She continued. "At first it was just slaps to my arms or my face, then he became more forceful and the slaps turned into punches."

Thad thought he might be sick. How could any man even think about raising his hand to a woman, let alone doing it? He felt a strong need to apologize for what the worst of his gender had apparently put her through. "I'm so sorry, Carrie," he said, taking her hands in his.

"You'd think I would have had the sense to get away from him after the first time," she murmured, her tone subdued. "But every time I tried to end things with him, I ended up with a black eye, a broken bone or stitches." She shook her head. "I'm ashamed to admit it, but I was terrified of him. I never knew what would set him off. I was afraid to let anyone know what he was doing to me because I knew I'd pay for it if he found out."

Thad's chest hurt from the viselike tightening around his ribs. The more he heard, the more sick it made him feel. Emotion threatened to choke him at the thought of the paralyzing fear she must have experienced, the intense pain of the jerk's repeated blows that she'd had little chance of fending off.

The room suddenly felt like a vacuum with no sense of time, no air to breathe and no sound beyond the pounding of his own heart. With sudden clarity he understood exactly why she'd reacted the way she had when he'd tackled her to keep her from being shot that first day up at Whisper Lake. A big man coming at her full force, taking her down and barking orders at her—even if they were orders intended to save her life—had triggered an episode of PTSD.

"Carrie, I am so sorry," he said, reaching to cup her cheek with his palm. "Please, forgive me for adding to your fears when we were up at Whisper Lake."

"You had no way of knowing." She shook her head and placed her hand over his where it rested along her jaw. "You were just trying to do what you've done since the moment we met. Protect me. If you hadn't been so persistent, I would have been killed, and it would have been a direct result of me allowing my fears to take over. I'm ashamed that I acted the way I did. I should be the one apologizing to you."

"There's no shame in fearing what you can't control, Carrie," he said, his voice rough with anger for what had happened to her. "How did you finally get away from Wilford?"

He thought the story would get better from here—that she'd tell him about a friend or family member who had helped her get away. To his horror, though, the story got worse as she described the night her ex-boyfriend had tried to choke her to death, and the terror he'd subjected her to while she was locked in the basement of his apartment building, awaiting his return to finish what he'd started.

Listening to her account, Thad felt like he was about to come unglued. That explained her insistence that she couldn't go down into a deep, dark, extremely damp root cellar up at the old lodge. He couldn't decide if the coil of pain inside of him was from anger at what the sorry excuse for a man had done to her or heartbreak for the physical and emotional pain she'd suffered and the terror that he knew for certain still haunted her.

"When I managed to escape, I went to the police. Chip was arrested, and almost a year to the day after the attack, he was sentenced to twenty years in prison for attempted murder."

"Is he still incarcerated?" If not, Chip Wilford was going to move up to the top spot on his personal list of suspects for all the recent attacks.

Carrie shook her head. "A little over a year ago, he was stabbed in the abdomen during an altercation with another inmate in the prison yard. The shiv pierced his aorta and there was nothing anyone could do. He bled out within a few minutes."

A wave of relief washed over him, followed closely by a good amount of guilt. He wasn't proud of his initial reaction. A man had lost his life and that should never be dismissed as insignificant or the source of satisfaction. *God, please forgive me for being pleased by the news that a man is dead. Although he had gone astray, he was still Your child.*

"How does all this tie in with something your dad found out?" he asked.

"Apparently, Chip's mother found a veritable arsenal in her basement, along with body armor and tactical gear," she answered. "She has two sons who are still living. One of them bought all of it. For whatever reason, she called the DA who prosecuted Chip to report it."

"Why didn't she just get in touch with local police or a county sheriff?" Thad asked, more confused than ever.

"I'm not sure, but I suspect she wasn't thinking clearly. She developed a form of dementia a few years ago, and her cognitive reasoning isn't always the best." She shook her head. "She might have thought the lawyer would have more sympathy for their situation and would be able to get through to her son or sons before they actually broke the law."

He nodded. "That sounds like a reasonable explanation."

"But I can't imagine either of Chip's brothers, Milo or Steve, doing anything like what's been happening. I got along well with their entire family, and they all assured me they didn't hold my testimony in Chip's trial against me."

He didn't want to say anything without proof, but people could change their opinions once they had time to step back and think about a situation. "How old are the Wilford brothers now?"

"Steve is three years older than me, so he just turned thirty last week and Milo… Oh, goodness, I can't believe it, but he's eighteen," she said, shaking her head. "Time flies and it's hard to think of him being this old. The last time I saw them was during the trial. Steve had just graduated from college, and Milo was getting ready to start middle school. As far as I know, Steve still lives at home to oversee his mother's care since her diagnosis of dementia. Milo is probably still at home, as well, since he would have graduated high school a few months ago."

"Where is Mr. Wilford?"

"He passed away from a brain aneurysm

a year or so before I met Chip." She sighed. "Milo was especially close to his dad, and from what Mrs. Wilford told me, he had a hard time dealing with his father's passing."

Thad didn't say anything, but his money was on the younger Wilford brother being behind the attempts to kill Carrie. When he'd seen the shooter that day up at Whisper Lake, he'd judged the guy to be late teens or early twenties. But he wasn't going to make accusations just yet. It was clear Carrie didn't want to think either of the brothers had anything to do with the attacks, and without proof, there was no sense in upsetting her. But all of the pieces fit for Thad. A boy who had been through a pair of troubling losses—first the death of the father he was close to and then his brother going to prison and dying, as well—could easily turn bitter and resentful. Especially when he had lived with the stigma of his brother being a convicted felon.

Deciding that Carrie needed a break from the heaviness of the past and the uncertainty of the situation they now faced, he stood up and tugged her to her feet to loosely wrap his arms around her waist. Grinning down at her, he couldn't resist asking, "Care Bear, huh?"

She blushed and rolled her eyes as she

rested her forehead against his chest. "My dad gave me that nickname when I was a baby."

Placing his index finger beneath her chin, he lifted her head until their gazes met. "I like it, Care Bear."

His grin faded as he tucked a strand of her long blond hair behind her ear. Staring down at her, he wanted nothing more than to kiss her, to press his lips to hers and find out for himself if they were as soft and sweet as he anticipated. Before he could think of all the reasons he shouldn't act on that thought, he lowered his head and brushed her mouth with his.

They were even softer and sweeter than he'd imagined. He expected her to push him away and read him the riot act for taking advantage of her when she was the most vulnerable. His pulse thundered in his ears when she reached up to wrap her arms around his neck, encouraging him to deepen the kiss.

The sound of someone clearing their throat was like a bucket of cold water being dumped over his head. "If you're not too…um…busy, I need to talk to you about something, little brother," Sean said, his voice tinged with humor.

"Give me a minute and I'll meet you in the kitchen," Thad answered without taking his gaze away from Carrie. Resting his forehead on hers, he took a deep breath. He owed her an apology. She deserved that, even if he couldn't truly bring himself to feel remorse for the best kiss he'd ever experienced. "I'm really sorry, Carrie. I shouldn't have done that, and I won't let it happen again."

Her eyes widened a moment before she pulled away from him, crossed her arms as if she was upset, then shook her head. "You don't owe me an apology. Just go find out what your brother wants to talk over with you."

He stared in bewilderment for several long seconds, then turned and walked from the room. He'd done the right thing by telling her he was sorry for taking advantage of her vulnerability, hadn't he? Or was she upset because his brother had witnessed the kiss? Or had he said or done something else that had offended her?

Thad blew out a frustrated breath as he walked across the great room to the kitchen area. He shouldn't be surprised by her reaction. His awkwardness around women had started when he was in high school, and in the following years, it hadn't gotten any better. He was always saying or doing the wrong thing, and he should know by now that acting on impulse or voicing his thoughts would get him into a heap of trouble with a woman. That was the way it happened every time.

Walking past his brother seated at the kitchen table, Thad went over to the counter to pour himself a cup of coffee, then joined Sean. "So what's going on?"

"I found several trail cameras positioned around the ranch yard and the rehab compound," Sean said, his expression grim. "And they weren't the kind you pick up in a hunting or fishing store. These had to have come from a place that sells the high-tech stuff. They don't just take still pictures. They send a live feed to whoever has a computer or cell phone with a compatible app. Every move you and Carrie made outside this house was being closely monitored by someone until I took them down and destroyed this jerk's little spy network."

ELEVEN

Carrie couldn't believe Thad had kissed her, couldn't believe that she'd encouraged him to deepen the kiss and couldn't believe that he'd felt compelled to apologize for it. But as she sat down behind his desk and stared at his computer screen, she had to admit she wasn't certain who she was the most upset with. Herself for encouraging him to kiss her instead of immediately putting a stop to it… or him for regretting the most exciting kiss of her entire life.

She propped her elbow on the desk's highly polished mahogany surface and rested her cheek in the palm of her hand. It didn't matter who had done or said what. Thad was definitely right about one thing. It was absolutely not going to happen again. She trusted Thad, but she'd also trusted Chip in the beginning and look where that had gotten her. No, she couldn't rely on her judgment when it came to men. If she did let down her guard and handed that kind of trust to anyone again, it just might get her killed.

"Carrie, could you join me and Sean in the kitchen?"

When she looked up, Thad hovered in the doorway, looking about as uncomfortable as she felt. "What's going on?" she asked, wondering—no, dreading—what had happened this time. Were they going to tell her she'd become more trouble than they wanted to deal with? Did they intend to ask her to leave Cougar Mountain?

"I think we're going to have to go to plan B," he said, waiting for her to walk with him to join his brother.

He held the chair for her, and once she was seated at the table, he filled a cup with coffee and set it in front of her. "I'm assuming that something's happened to warrant a *plan B*?" she asked, directing her question to Sean. She wasn't ready to meet Thad's gaze any more than he seemed to be ready to meet hers.

"I found some surveillance cameras around the ranch yard and up at the rehab compound. They're motion activated and capable of live streaming to a cell phone or computer." He took a sip of his coffee. "It's how this guy has known whenever you and Thad leave the house and the direction you've gone."

"This sounds like something right out of a spy movie. What does this mean?" she asked, incredulously. "Is he a government agent or just someone willing to spend a fortune on spy equipment in order to keep track of me?"

"Sean and I discussed that and we're sure it's the latter," Thad answered. "We know he's persistent, but he's also given the impression that he's pulling out all the stops in his effort to keep an eye on your whereabouts."

"In other words, he's stalking me with an intent to kill—and he's willing to shell out whatever it takes to get the job done." Putting it into words sent an involuntary shudder through the entire length of her body, and she had to take a deep breath to settle her frayed nerves.

"We're going to see that he doesn't get the chance," Thad said, reaching over to cover her hand with his where it rested on the table.

Every time he touched her, it felt as if his strength became hers, like they were truly a team and in this nightmare together. Which was absolutely ridiculous, all things considered. They hadn't known each other more than a handful of days. But in that short length of time, they'd escaped death together more times than she wanted to count. "What do you have in mind?"

"I have a cabin not far from the mountain's peak," Sean said, setting his cup on the table. "It's off the grid and it's unlikely this guy is aware that it even exists. You and Thad should be safe up there, while the rest of us assist law enforcement in searching every part of this mountain to find where he's hiding so he can be taken into custody."

"We figure since he's been watching this part of the mountain, he hasn't had the time or the inclination to explore things up at the summit," Thad added.

She nodded. "I get that. But how is this cabin safe when it's off the grid? If he does find us, there would be no way for us to get in touch with anyone." She couldn't understand how that would be safer than staying at the ranch with more people around. Watching the men exchange a knowing smile, she frowned. "What aren't you telling me about this place?"

"You know Sean is former FBI, right?" Thad grinned when she nodded. "He has a state-of-the-art security system at the cabin, along with electricity, hot and cold running water and a satellite phone and internet system. Everything is run on solar power, and there's a filtration system that keeps everything environmentally friendly."

"And you consider that *off the grid*?" she asked, certain that her eyes reflected her surprise.

Sean laughed. "I built it with the idea of it being a retreat—a place to relax and take pictures of wildlife without giving up any of the creature comforts we all know and love."

"That's great, but how do we get there without him knowing which direction we've gone?" she asked, turning to Thad. "We can't hike up there without him following us. Is there a road? How would that be any different? He could still follow us."

"Nope, no road. But we've got things covered," he answered, smiling. "Sean has a helicopter and a license to fly it. He's going to take us up there. When it's safe to come down from the cabin, or when we need to escape any danger that arises, he'll come and get us."

"We'll take off like we're heading east to Cheyenne and then double back to come around the southern end of the mountain and fly up the west face to the cabin," Sean explained.

"In other words, the scenic route," Carrie said, warming to the idea. As long as she had a laptop and internet access, she'd still be able to search for information that might lead to the perpetrator behind this madness. "I'm in. When are we going to do this? And do I have time to send someone to purchase a laptop for me?"

"I've got one you can borrow," Sean offered. "Unless, of course, you want your own."

"Your laptop will be fine. Thank you, I really appreciate it."

"Can you be ready in an hour to take off?" Thad asked, taking his and her cups to the sink to rinse and place in the dishwasher.

Nodding, she rose to her feet to head toward the guest room to gather her things, but stopped suddenly. "What about your office hours at the veterinary clinic?" she asked. "I know you weren't able to open at the end of last week. I don't want to keep you from taking care of your patients."

"Don't worry about it. My vet tech is taking over for me today, and I'll have her run things for the rest of the week," he said, shrugging.

"She's great—I have complete confidence that she can handle anything that comes up until I get back into the office. If there is anything she can't do or doesn't feel comfortable handling herself, or if it's an emergency situation, the owners can take their pets to Cheyenne for more immediate attention."

"If you're sure…"

"I am." His smile caused her pulse to race as he took her hands in his. "We're going to see this through to the end, Carrie. Together."

A warmth spread throughout her body and her heart sped up. She forgot all about being upset with him. All she could think about was the way his kiss had affected her earlier and how she wanted him to kiss her again. "I'll… uh, be ready to go as soon as I get packed," she finally managed as she pulled away and hurried from the room.

She'd told herself that she couldn't trust any man, that where men were concerned her judgment wasn't sound—and for seven years, she'd believed that. But somehow Thad Hanson had breached her defenses. He made her want to believe that he was different, that there were still good guys in the world, ones who respected women and didn't want to crush their hopes and dreams.

Placing her clothes into the backpack she'd bought at the Rancher's General Store, she shook her head. She'd tried to keep her wits about her, but she was beginning to think she'd been fighting a losing battle from the moment they met. She was falling for Thad Hanson, and no matter how much she tried to resist, there didn't seem to be a thing she could do to stop herself.

"That's Whisper Lake down there," Thad said, speaking to Carrie through the headsets his brother had handed them when they got into the helicopter. The sight of the picturesque lake below never failed to remind him how blessed he was to live in such a beautiful area. The water reflected the surrounding mountains like a huge mirror, and when the weather was calm, like it was today, every detail was captured in the awe-inspiring image.

"This is amazing," she said, her voice filled with the same wonder he always felt when he flew with Sean over this area.

As he stared at the woman who was quickly becoming as important to him as the air he breathed, his chest tightened and he suddenly realized that what he'd felt for his college girl-friend didn't come close to what he felt for

Carrie. It didn't matter that he'd only known Carrie for a few days while he and Missy had been together for over two years. He knew in his heart that he was falling hard and fast for her. She was strong, intelligent and one of the most caring people he'd ever known. She loved working with animals, had made a career of protecting them and didn't look down on him for his dedication to their welfare. Had God sent her to the mountain for them to be together? They'd both been in relationships before that were hurtful and left them with reasons to avoid becoming involved ever again. But the feelings he had for her were so strong that she overcame his resolve. Did Carrie feel the same way about him? Did he have the nerve to find out?

"We'll be landing up at the cabin in about five minutes," his brother said, thankfully interrupting his thoughts. Sean moved the stick to bring the helicopter around for one last look at Whisper Valley before he flew them up toward the cabin at the summit. "The cabin is stocked with enough provisions to last a couple of weeks, so you should have plenty of everything you need. I doubt that it will take that long for us to catch this guy, but it's always better to have more than you need instead of not enough."

"I'm sure we'll be fine," Thad answered as the skids of the helicopter touched down in the meadow in front of the cabin.

"When you called this place a cabin, I was expecting something a lot more rustic. This looks like a full-time residence instead of a wilderness retreat," Carrie said as Thad hopped out of the chopper, then helped her out. Picking up their backpacks, they walked with Sean toward the cabin.

"After I left the FBI and started photographing wildlife, I spent several weeks at a time up here building the cabin," Sean explained as they climbed the cabin steps and he unlocked the padlock on the thick, solid wood door. He laughed as he added, "I quickly figured out that at the end of the day I wanted a hot shower, ice for a glass of tea and a king-size bed. That's when I started working to make it what it is today."

"I'm sure your wife loves it," she said, smiling.

"She hasn't complained so far," he said, grinning. Sean turned back toward the steps. "Thad, while you get your and Carrie's gear stowed away, I'll go out to the shed and make sure everything is up and running. Make yourselves at home, and I'll join you in a few minutes."

Opening the door, Thad stepped back for her to precede him. Once she crossed the threshold and he came in to stand beside her, he smiled at the surprise on her pretty face. "The inside is even more beautiful than the outside," she said, walking over to stare at some of the pictures his brother had taken of wildlife on the mountain.

"Sean put in the work to make it what he wanted, and we all donated our time helping out as we could," he said, leading the way up the stairs to the second floor. "There are three bedrooms and two baths up here and another bathroom downstairs, so I thought you could have the master suite and I'll take the guest room closest to the stairs. Sound good to you?"

"Fine, but I'm more than willing to take the other guest room," she offered.

"Nope." He continued on down the hallway to the master bedroom to place her backpack on the bench at the end of the bed. "Sean and I talked it over and we agreed that this is the most secure room. There's a lock on the door, as well as a lock on the adjoining bathroom door. If Drone Jerk gets inside, he'll have to get through me at the head of the stairs to get to you. On the off chance that happens, he'll have two locked doors to go through after that, and if you have your gun you've got a decent chance of shooting him before he can shoot you."

"That makes sense." She rubbed her upper arms with both hands, and he knew she was probably chilled by the thought.

Setting his backpack on the floor, he reached out and took her into his arms. "It's just a precaution. The chances of anything like that happening are slim to none. As far as we know, this guy doesn't know this cabin is up here. And if he does manage to find us, we should find out in plenty of time to get away. Sean installed a state-of-the-art security system. A rabbit can't even twitch his nose without setting it off, and believe me, when it goes off, it's loud enough in here to wake a dead man."

When she nodded and burrowed closer to his chest, he held her against him for a few minutes, then, deciding she'd feel better if he was to show her how the security system worked, he pulled away and led her down the hall to the room he would use. After placing his bag on the bed, he guided her downstairs.

"Where are we going?" she asked as they descended the steps.

"The command room," he said. They crossed the living area and stopped at the door, on the opposite side of the kitchen. "Get ready for a security setup that James Bond would be proud of." Opening the door, he flipped on the overhead light in the windowless room. "Once it's all turned on, the motion-activated cameras send a live feed to these eight monitors. Whenever something triggers it, an alarm goes off and alerts us that someone or something has breached the perimeter."

"This is…" The sound of an alarm caused her to jump. "Oh, goodness! That is loud."

He turned off the warning and pointed to one of the flat screens. "Sean just stepped out of the utility shed and is heading back to the house."

She grinned. "You weren't joking about the state-of-the-art system. Why did he think he needed so much security up here?"

Thad grinned. "For one thing, he's former FBI and will tell you there's no such thing as too much security. And for another, he uses this system to get some of his pictures. When an animal crosses the perimeter as it's taking a stroll through the meadow, Sean has the option to either step outside or open a window and capture the image before the animal is even aware it's close to a human."

"What about at night? Don't they shy away from the lights of the cabin?" she asked as they walked back into the kitchen.

"Blackout curtains." He shrugged. "It keeps the four-legged as well as the two-legged critters from knowing this cabin is even here."

"I think you two are all set," Sean said, entering the cabin. "If you need anything just give me a call on the sat phone."

When his brother turned to go, Thad followed him out. "Thanks for loaning us the cabin."

"Anytime, little brother." Sean started down the steps, but turned back. "If you want to get out and show Carrie some of the sights up here, there's a nesting pair of golden eagles just over the peak, not far from Mountain Goat Rock. I've been photographing them for a couple of years. So far they've raised four eaglets in that nest. It's a sight well worth seeing. Just watch your surroundings and keep an eye out for unwanted company."

"Will do," Thad said, smiling. "Carrie's

going to love seeing that. Thanks for giving me the heads-up."

"Take care and enjoy the time with your new girlfriend," Sean said, heading out to the chopper.

"She's not my girlfriend," Thad insisted, careful to keep his voice low. He didn't want Carrie hearing his brother's assumption. It would likely upset her, since he doubted she was open to the idea of anything more than friendship between them.

"Hey, if you'll remember I said the same thing last year when I was guarding Bailey. Look how that turned out," Sean said, grinning from ear to ear. "She's home right now, baking a cake for our three-month anniversary. It'll go great with my favorite supper that she's serving tonight."

Shaking his head, Thad pointed toward the helicopter. "Go home to your loving wife, and tell her my birthday's coming up in a couple of weeks and I haven't had any of her stuffed shells in a while."

Sean laughed and climbed into the pilot's seat. Thad watched as his brother started the rotor blades spinning, and in no time, the bird lifted up and flew up over the top of the peak, disappearing from sight. He was glad that his brother had shared the news about the nesting eagles. As a wildlife rehabber and an avid animal enthusiast, he was looking forward to seeing the majestic birds, and he knew Carrie would be just as happy.

Walking back into the cabin, he found her poking around in the pantry to see what they could have for supper. "Carrie, how would you like to go see a pair of golden eagles tomorrow?"

TWELVE

The following morning when Carrie adjusted her binoculars, her breath caught at the sight of the golden eagles lazily gliding on the air currents high above. "This is absolutely breathtaking, Thad. Thank you for bringing me up here. I wouldn't have wanted to miss this."

They'd hiked about a half mile from the cabin up to the peak and down the east side to the cliff with the nest.

"I can't take all the credit," he said, lowering his own binoculars. "Sean told me the eagles were up here and where to find them."

Looking through the field glasses, she noticed one of the eagles was soaring toward the rocks where the huge, bowl-shaped nest rested among a cluster of rocks beneath an overhang. When the big bird landed on the raised side of the nest, she understood why Thad's brother Sean loved taking pictures of them. Dark brown in color with a golden sheen on their heads and backs, the raptors were both fierce looking and majestic at the same time. With a piercing "don't mess with me or I'll end you" gaze and an occasional high-pitched cry, they were undeniably intimidating and absolutely beautiful.

Caught up in the moment of observing the magnificent birds of prey, she gasped when Thad's arm shot out to wrap around her waist, capturing her in a viselike grip and instantly pulling her to a lower stance. "There's someone on the ridge across from us with a rifle scope," he said, keeping his voice low. "I saw a glint of light off the lens of the scope and I know it's not one of my brothers. They would have told us if they were coming. I have a hunch that's Drone Jerk right over there."

"That ridge is part of this mountain, isn't it?" she whispered, her heart speeding up at the thought of having to run for her life yet again. Hiding, wondering if no matter where she went or what she did, someone would always be out there watching her, biding his time while he waited for his chance to kill her. It was beginning to wear on her nerves.

"Do you think he's seen us?" she asked, praying this wasn't going to be her life from now on.

"I'm almost positive he has." He'd barely got the words out when the high-pitched whine of a bullet and the sharp report of a rifle had them flattening themselves on top of the rock ledge they'd kneeled on to view the eagles.

"How does he keep finding us?" she asked, unable to keep her voice from wobbling.

"I don't know." Thad's arm tightened around her, and he kissed the top of her head. "It's going to be all right, Carrie. I promise. He's over there on that ridge and we're over here. Yes, it's part of the same mountain, but it's still not quick or easy to head from there to here. It's going to take him a while to get over here. By the time he does, we'll be on the other side of the peak, back inside the safety of the cabin." Thad urged her to belly crawl backward until they were away from the slight rise at the edge of the ledge. "He can't see us now and won't know where we've gone, even if he does go higher where the entire ledge is visible."

"Because we'll be long gone," she said, feeling more confident with Thad by her side.

She wasn't going to analyze that fact because she wasn't ready to acknowledge just exactly what it might mean.

He leaned over to press a kiss to her forehead, then took her by the hand. "Ready?"

She nodded. "Let's go."

Allowing him to lead her away from the ledge, they quickly walked along a natural path between several boulders before they started making the uphill trek toward the peak. The trees at the top of Cougar Mountain were few and sometimes far between, but they were Colorado blue spruce, extremely tall with a wide spread of branches at the base. Since their tormentor had to hike down from the ridge and then up toward the summit, they had the advantage of time, as well as fairly good cover.

"I hate to ask this, but do you think you could brave a tunnel?" Thad asked when they reached the trees.

"Why?"

"If we take the detour, it will get us back to the cabin about forty-five minutes faster," he explained. "But if it's going to bother you or you don't think you can do it, we can forget that idea. We'll be fine going the long way."

Walking beside him, she glanced up at

his handsome face. She wasn't certain why, but being with him, knowing that he would move the very mountain they stood on in his effort to keep her safe, seemed to give her more courage than she'd had in the past seven years.

"It might bother me, but not enough to keep me from trying it," she said decisively. Just knowing that the jerk had seen them, shot at them and was no doubt doing his best to catch up to them at that very moment, she wanted to get back to the security of the cabin as quickly as they could. *Lord, please help me do this. Please help me finally conquer some of this paralyzing fear.*

Thad's smile lit the darkest, most insecure regions of her heart. "I've got faith that you'll be fine. And I promise you won't be inside the tunnel alone. God will be with you and so will I. One of my favorite scriptures is Philippians 4:13. 'I can do all things through Christ who strengthens me.'"

Thad's faith humbled her and she knew he was right. God had been with her that night in the dark, wet basement in Chip's apartment building and He was with her now. "Absolutely."

They had just crossed the peak and started

down the other side when Thad steered her over to the left of the trail. They came to a grouping of different-sized boulders interspersed with huge spruce trees against the cliff face. She quickly looked around to see if there was a reason they needed to hide or take shelter among the giant rocks. She found none and was just about to ask if there was danger she was unaware of, when he pushed some low-hanging spruce branches aside to reveal a padlocked door made of iron bars blocking the entrance to a dark tunnel in the rock wall.

"This must be a really long tunnel," she murmured, staring into the dark hole, her courage slipping a notch.

"It's a little more than a hundred and fifty yards," he said, his tone as gentle and reassuring as it had been when he'd talked to the injured mare she'd watched him treat. When she looked at him, his warm, understanding smile reinforced her determination. "Don't force yourself if you don't think you can do it, Carrie. You shouldn't feel pressured in any way. I want this to be your choice."

"As long as God and you are with me, I can do this," she said, realizing she drew strength just by stating the truth aloud.

He kissed the top of her head, then reached into his jeans pocket to remove a set of keys. Opening the lock, he pulled the door open and stepped back for her to enter, following her into the mouth of the tunnel before turning and securing the door behind them. He took her by the hand and, using a flashlight from his backpack, lit their way. "We'll be back inside the cabin before you know it."

"Was this tunnel already here or did your brother blast through the rock to make it?" she asked, noticing there weren't any supports or beams holding it up.

"It's actually a branch off of a natural cave that Sean discovered when he was digging footings for the cabin's foundation," Thad explained.

"So where does the cave go? Is there another way out?" She kept asking questions because the sound of his voice answering them seemed to keep her anxiety from escalating to a full-blown panic attack as they continued going down the long, narrow corridor.

"This tunnel curved away and joined the main part of the cave about twenty feet from the cabin, so Sean sealed off this section, adjusted his plans to build the cabin over it and installed a trapdoor in the command room."

"I didn't notice one yesterday when you showed me around." She marveled at his brother's resourcefulness. "Leave it to a former FBI agent to take advantage of an opportunity to have a secret escape."

He laughed. "As it turned out, it's a good thing he did." Thad shrugged as they entered the underground room Sean had added at the end of the tunnel. "This is the second time it's proved to be useful." He shone the light at a sturdy-looking built-in metal ladder that reached all the way up to the top of the tunnel. "I'm going to go up to unlock the deadbolt and open the trapdoor. I promise it will only take me a minute, and then I'll climb back down. You'll be up and out of here in no time at all."

When Carrie climbed up the ladder and came out through the door in the floor of the command room minutes later, she was not only relieved to be back within the safety of the beautiful cabin, she also felt a sense of accomplishment that she hadn't expected. She'd walked over a hundred and fifty yards through a dark, damp tunnel and hadn't had a meltdown. *Thank You, Lord, for hearing my prayer and for sending this wonderful man to help me.*

* * *

As soon as Thad locked the trapdoor and replaced the braided rug used to cover it, he radioed Sean to let him know that Drone Jerk had been on the ridge across from the golden eagle's nest. While Carrie went into the kitchen to poke around for something to make for supper, he and Sean had discussed whether they should evacuate from the cabin. It was decided that since it was late afternoon, Sean would fly up first thing in the morning to bring them back down to Thad's part of the ranch.

"Do you want me to help you make supper?" he asked, walking into the kitchen where she had something that smelled amazing bubbling in a pot on top of the stove.

"Do you know how to peel potatoes?" she asked.

"Of course," he said, frowning. "Why wouldn't I?"

"Well, you let me know that first evening at your brother's house that cooking wasn't a part of your skillset," she said, laughing.

"Peeling potatoes is one thing," he said, grinning. "Cooking them is another thing entirely."

"Then grab a knife, don't cut yourself and peel a few medium-size potatoes."

"Don't cut myself?" he grumbled. "I'll have you know that I'm very skilled with a scalpel."

"You're pretty good with a needle and sutures, too, but that doesn't mean you're a tailor."

He threw back his head and laughed. "Good point."

As he washed the potatoes, he couldn't help but think how he could get used to the two of them working together like this, making a meal to share every evening. But no sooner had he had the thought than a jolt of reality as strong as an electric cattle prod raced through him. What was he thinking? Carrie wasn't interested in anything more from him than friendship. Sure, she hadn't objected when he kissed her forehead this afternoon as they were trying to get back to the cabin after being shot at. But that could easily be explained. They'd been shocked by the presence of the jerk on the ridge across from them, and she had been preoccupied with trying to overcome her fear of entering Sean's secret tunnel. It was depressing to admit it, but it probably hadn't even registered with her that his lips had even come close to her.

He'd just turned his head to glance at her stirring the pot of stew on the stove when his phone emitted a loud rhythmic noise that caused him and Carrie both to jump. His heart pounded against his ribs as he turned off the warning alarm on the phone app connecting him to the cabin's security system and wiped his hands on a towel. He didn't have cell service, but the cabin's network allowed the app on his phone to interact with the security system. He crossed the kitchen to the door of the command room to check the bank of monitors.

"Is someone out there?" Carrie asked, following close behind him.

"Something or someone crossed the perimeter," he said, keeping his voice low. "It's probably just a raccoon or some other animal out for a moonlight stroll." Staring into each screen, he spotted a bobcat sauntering into view on the south side of the meadow. Feeling some of the tension that gripped him ease, he glanced at the other monitors to make sure nothing else was prowling around when his heart stopped, and he leaned forward to make sure he wasn't hallucinating.

A man in fatigues with a tactical backpack, carrying a rifle and wearing a sidearm in a holster at his waist, walked into view from the east. Thad would stake his reputation on the man being Drone Jerk. He was equally sure that the man's backpack was loaded with extra rounds of ammunition, as well as what was probably a slew of other unpleasant surprises of the firearms type.

"Thad?"

He raised his index finger to his lips. "He's about fifty yards from the front porch. We need to be extremely quiet. Maybe he'll think the house is unoccupied." He pointed toward the lamp at the end of the couch in the great room. "Kill that light and go upstairs to the master suite."

"He can't see through the blackout curtains, right?" she asked, turning off the stew she'd been making and quickly switching off the kitchen lights.

"No, but I don't want to take the chance there's a gap between the panels."

"Where are you going to be?" she asked as he followed her.

"I'll be down here in case he manages to get inside." While she turned off the lamp by the couch, he continued on to the fireplace where his rifle rested on the gun rack above the mantel. Taking it down, he made sure there was a round in the chamber and the safety was off. "The windows are bullet-proof glass, so he probably won't be able to get in that way. The door is even sturdier— six inches of solid wood with a metal plate on the inside surface. But nothing is foolproof, and I'm not taking any chances." He reached for the box of rifle slugs he'd placed on the mantel when they arrived the day before. "If he makes it through, I'm going to aim for his leg to take him down."

He watched her retrieve her gun from where it lay on top of the mantel and an extra clip of ammunition. "If you're staying down here, I'm staying with you," she whispered. "You'll need backup, and I'm not leaving you down here by yourself when I'm perfectly capable of helping."

Before he could argue with her, he heard the sound of someone in big, heavy boots clomping across the porch. Guns drawn, they took up their positions behind the kitchen island as they waited to see what their assailant's next move was going to be.

When Drone Jerk banged on the door several times, Thad whispered close to her ear,

"Stay as quiet as you can no matter what he does." Something struck one of the windows next to the door, and Thad figured the man had used the butt of his rifle to try breaking through. He rested his rifle on the top of the island and aimed it toward the door. He fully expected the guy to try firing through it next. "Go into the command room and use the sat phone to get hold of Sean. Tell him what's going on and advise him that we need him to bring the helicopter up here to pick us up ASAP."

THIRTEEN

When Carrie made the call, Sean promised help would be there as quickly as possible. The sound of a rifle slug embedding itself in the front door caused her to add, "Hurry. He's trying to shoot through the door now."

Crawling back to Thad, they stayed down as the shooter fired twice more. Fortunately, he must not have had armor piercing rounds because the slugs hadn't penetrated past the steel plate. As they waited for another shot, the sound of heavy boots crossed the porch and descended the steps. Then there was silence.

"Has he left?" she asked quietly.

"We might have sold him on the idea that the cabin is unoccupied," Thad answered. "But at this point, I'm not counting on anything. He could very easily have retreated to the trees to watch for us to give our presence away. Or maybe he's going to try to enter another way."

She nodded. "I was thinking the same thing." A sudden thought caused a cold dread to rush through her. "Will your brother be all right landing his helicopter in the meadow with this jerk still out there? Do you think he'll try to shoot the helicopter or Sean?"

"I can guarantee that Sean won't come alone. He's going to bring my brothers and probably several members of law enforcement. I don't think this guy is going to want to add that many more to the list of people he'll need to eliminate because they witnessed some of his crimes," Thad said, shaking his head.

"But you and I will still be in danger," she stated.

Thad nodded. "He's not going to give up on trying to take us out." When she raised an eyebrow, he explained, "He's shooting at you because you're his primary target and he's shooting at me because I witnessed what he's done. Plus the fact that he's probably pretty angry with me for shooting down his flying toy."

"The drone."

He nodded. "I got a good look at that thing after I shot it down. It wasn't a cheap model a hobbyist would have just to play around with. It was an expensive top-of-the-line drone that's used by professionals in the media, on movie sets and by first responders when they're searching for someone."

They fell silent and she thought about his observance. She wanted to reject the idea that any of Chip's family could have anything to do with her current problems, but the circumstantial evidence kept piling up. They *did* have motive. She was responsible for their brother going to prison where he ended up dying. They were also well-off and had the money to purchase high-end items like the drone, expensive firearms and tactical gear, as well as the sophisticated spy cameras Sean had found around Thad's house and the rehab center's compound. She drew in a steadying breath. There was only one way to know for sure.

"Thad?" When he looked up, she asked, "Does the security system record whenever something triggers the motion-activated cameras?"

He nodded. "The recordings are available for a week before they're automatically erased, unless they're manually saved for some reason." His dark brown gaze met and held hers as understanding dawned. "If it's one of Wilford's brothers, you're thinking that you might recognize this guy, right?"

Both of them rose to their feet and hurried into the security room. Thad manually saved an extra copy of the video and ran it back to the moment the alarm was activated. As he worked, Carrie wiped her cold clammy palms on the legs of her jeans. She wanted all of this to end, to free her from having to constantly look over her shoulder, but she truly didn't want either of the remaining Wilford brothers to be involved. She feared it would be the end of their mother. How much could the fragile thread tethering her to reality withstand before it broke? From what she'd heard, the woman did have moments of clarity interspersed with the cloudiness of her dementia, but would something like this send her into a downward spiral?

"Okay, I've got it set to start at the moment he stepped out of the trees into the meadow. It runs until he left the porch and headed up toward the summit to the east." He moved the desk chair and motioned for her to take a seat. "It's pretty much like any video on the internet. Click on the arrow to start, or click on the back button to replay a section you want to rewatch. If you want to freeze the image, just click pause."

She nodded and sighed heavily, her hand hovering over the mouse. "It's going to be difficult for me, whether it's one of the Wilfords or not."

"I understand," he said, his tone gentle. "Would you like for me to leave and give you some space to watch it alone?"

Reaching up, she took hold of his hand. "No, please stay. I think I'm going to need the moral support."

His understanding smile and the reassuring touch of his large hand wrapped around hers gave her the strength and courage she needed. Clicking the mouse activated the surveillance video, and she watched the male figure walk across the meadow toward the porch. At first, she couldn't say for certain if she'd ever seen him before. But restarting the recording, Carrie caught a moment where the man turned his head toward the camera he wasn't aware had been capturing his every move. Pausing it to freeze the image, she stared at the man's face for several long moments. He looked familiar, but it was only when she noticed the cowlick at the edge of his forehead causing his unruly hair to sweep to one side and the thin white scar that bisected his left eyebrow, a mark left from an accident while learning to ride his bicycle, that her breath caught on a soft sob. She hadn't seen him in over seven years and he'd grown a lot from the eleven-year-old he'd been at the end of the trial, but without question she was staring at the grown-up version of Milo Wilford, Chip's youngest brother.

"Do you recognize him?" Thad asked, kneeling beside the desk chair. He couldn't be sure, but she'd tightened her grip on his hand and he thought he heard her catch her breath.

When she turned to look at him, the tears filling her eyes just about did him in. "I don't want to believe it, but I can't deny it anymore. Milo Wilford is the person trying to kill us."

"I'm so sorry, Carrie," he said, gathering her into his arms. He hated to see her so shaken. It had to be devastating to learn that someone she knew and used to view as a little brother despised her so much that he wanted to see her dead. But at the same time, he couldn't deny it was a relief to finally know who had been stalking them. Now that they had a name, they were closer to catching him, closer to learning the reason behind his senseless vendetta and closer to stopping him for good.

But even as he thought about how much it would mean for Carrie to finally be free to live her life without fear and how much he wanted that for her, he couldn't help but dread her going back to her life in Eagle Fork, while he stayed on Cougar Mountain and got used to being without her. It was going to be especially hard with her so close and running into her occasionally around town.

"Why would Milo do this?" she asked. "His mother told me after the trial that he was angry with Chip for hurting me. How could he have changed so much?"

"I don't know." As he continued to hold her, he heard the sound of Sean's helicopter approaching. "Sean is almost here," he said, stroking her hair as he cradled her to him. "I'm sure now that we have a name to give him and someone for the authorities to focus on, you'll get the answers you need to move past this."

"I—I...hope...so," she said, swiping at her cheeks. "I want answers, but it's going to be hard to hear him admit that he wanted to kill me."

"Maybe he'll plead guilty and save you from having to testify."

He rose to his feet and disarmed the alarm to keep it from going off when Sean touched down in the meadow. When he heard the sound of a couple more choppers arriving, he pulled her up from the chair, kissed the top of her head and held her to his side before heading toward the door. "We need to tell Sean who they're searching for and the direction he went when he left."

"I'll make a pot of coffee," Carrie offered, walking over to the kitchen counter. "I don't think I'll be able to sleep tonight, anyway, and I'm sure whoever your brother brought with him will start searching for Milo right away. The least I can do is have coffee ready for them."

"I'll be back as soon as I talk to Sean," Thad said as he crossed the great room to open the door. Noticing the dents in the steel plate on the inside surface of the door, he didn't think he'd ever been more grateful that his oldest brother was a stickler for details. If that sheet of steel hadn't been added to the door after Sean guarded Bailey a year ago,

Milo Wilford might have been more success-ful in blasting his way through it.

"Are you two all right?" Sean asked as he and Blane climbed the steps to meet Thad on the porch.

"Where's Carrie?" Blane asked.

"We're fine. She's inside making coffee. She's shook up, but I think that has more to do with her recognizing the shooter on the se-curity video than him trying to shoot through the door," Thad said, noticing the chunks of oak the bullets had carved out of the wooden side of the door.

"Who was it? One of the Wilford boys?" Sean asked.

Thad nodded. "The younger one—Milo Wilford. He took off up the trail toward the peak about a half hour ago."

"I'll go tell the DCI's lead detective," Sean said, jogging down the steps toward the dozen or so men climbing out of the two large he-licopters.

"How did the Department of Criminal In-vestigation get here so fast?" Thad asked.

"They decided to concentrate their search on Cougar Mountain because that's where there have been the most sightings of Wil-ford." Blane shrugged. "They've moved into the bunkhouses on mine and Sean's sections of the ranch."

"I'll bet our former FBI brother was the one who suggested it and offered the bunkhouse accommodations," Thad said, raising an eyebrow.

Blane grinned. "Ding, ding, ding. You are correct, Dolittle."

When Sean returned to the cabin, they went inside to find Carrie sitting at the table, staring at the cup of coffee on the table in front of her. "Are you doing okay?" Thad asked, filling mugs with coffee for him and his brothers.

"I'll admit it was a shock at first to learn Milo was behind all of this," she answered, taking a sip. "But it's been years since I've seen him. There's really no telling what he's like these days. I have no idea what influences he had growing up or the effect his brother's incarceration and death had on him."

Thad pulled out the chair next to Carrie and sat down. "People change. Especially kids. Sometimes troubled kids get their acts together and other times good kids take a wrong turn."

"Thad's right," Blane agreed. "I used to work at a camp for troubled kids while I was in college. There were times the littlest thing was what sent a kid off the rails and landed him in trouble."

They were all silent for several minutes before Sean motioned toward the command room. "I think I'll go check the security footage."

"I've already saved the video to the hard drive, as well as a memory stick," Thad said as his brother got to his feet. "I figured it could be used as evidence when all this goes to trial."

"I'm proud of you, little brother." Sean grinned. "You're finally starting to think more like law enforcement than a veterinarian."

"In other words, there's hope for me yet?"

"Time will tell," Sean answered at the same time there was a knock on the door.

When Sean walked over to see who it was, a man with a DCI lanyard stepped into the great room. "Just wanted to let you all know that we tracked him to the peak and over to the east side of the mountain."

"You caught him?" Carrie asked.

The detective shook his head. "No, ma'am. We had him surrounded on a rock ledge, but instead of giving up, he jumped twenty feet to the bottom of a ravine, lay there a few seconds, then jumped up and limped off through the brush."

Thad watched her turn as pale as a blank sheet of paper. "So he's still on the loose?"

The man looked chagrined. "Yes, but I've got a team of twelve following him. We should have him in custody by morning. He's not moving too fast—we think his ankle is either sprained or broken."

Carrie's shoulders drooped and Thad knew how she felt. Milo Wilford was turning out to be as elusive as a shadow, and it was high time they finally pinned him down. He had chased them all over Cougar Mountain and whether Wilford was caught by morning or not, he and Carrie were going to return to his part of the ranch and make their stand to end this thing from there.

The following evening, Carrie was pleasantly surprised when Thad opened the back door of his ranch house to a parade of Hansons, carrying pans of Italian giant stuffed shells, a huge bowl of salad, platters piled high with garlic bread, a beautiful Italian cream cake and a gallon pail of homemade vanilla ice cream. Setting the food they carried on the counters, each one of Thad's brothers gave him a one-armed hug and a slap on the back as they wished him happy birthday. Not to be outdone, his father set two gallon jugs of iced tea beside the food and stepped forward to wrap his youngest son in a big bear hug. The affection Thad's family so easily displayed for each other was heart-warming and made her wish she was a part of this wonderful, loving clan instead of an outsider. She loved her family, but they didn't make a weekly habit of having a big family meal. In fact, the last time they'd gathered for a big family dinner had been last spring at Easter.

"Mind you, I'm not complaining," Thad said, laughing. "But what is this all about? My birthday isn't until the end of next week."

"Bailey and I decided to celebrate your birthday early. We also have a couple of big announcements we want to make," Mrs. Hanson said, placing the bowl of salad on the kitchen island before turning to kiss Thad on his cheek. When the woman turned toward Carrie, she walked up to wrap her in a moth-erly hug. "It's so good to see you again, Car-rie. I'm so thankful that you and Thad weren't hurt while you were up at Sean's cabin."

"Thank you, Mrs. Hanson," she said, hugging the woman back.

"Please call me Annie or Mom," the woman said, smiling. "Mrs. Hanson was my mother-in-law."

"Thank you, Annie."

Bailey joined them, giving her a hug, as well. "It's been several hours since the authorities lost track of the man responsible for all the trouble. How are you holding up?" The genuine concern on the pretty redhead's face had Carrie blinking back tears.

"I'm doing okay," she said, shrugging one shoulder. "Just waiting for the other shoe to drop."

Bailey smiled sympathetically. "I know how hard it has to be for you, waiting for him to be found. Sean said the consensus among the various branches of law enforcement is that he must be hiding out while his injured leg heals."

Carrie nodded. "The lead DCI detective said if it was just a sprain and not a broken bone, Milo Wilford should show up again within a few days."

Annie Hanson put one arm around Carrie's shoulders and the other around Bailey's. "I'm confident all of this will be over with soon and everyone will be safe." She smiled. "Now, no more talk of bad guys tonight. We're here to celebrate Thad's birthday and make a couple of exciting announcements, so let's get the table set and the party started."

"Sounds good to me," Bailey said, a radiant smile lighting her pretty face. "I'll pour the iced tea."

"I'm on the table settings," Carrie volunteered, opening one of the cabinet doors to reach for a stack of plates.

"I'll set up a buffet on the island," Mrs. Hanson said as she started arranging food along the black marble countertop.

Within minutes they all stood around the big, round dining table and joined hands. Mr. Hanson cleared his throat a moment before he prayed in his booming baritone. "Heavenly Father, thank You for this bountiful meal we are about to eat, and please bless those who prepared it. Lord, please keep us all safe in Your care and protect us from those who wish us harm. In Your Heavenly name we pray. Amen."

Levi and Blane remained standing while Mr. Hanson, Sean and Thad held the chairs for the women to be seated. In no time, Carrie was enjoying some of the most delicious food she could ever remember eating as she listened to the brothers tell stories about their childhood on Cougar Mountain. Once the meal was over, the brothers cleared away the dishes and made a pot of coffee. When they returned to the table, Bailey lit the candles on the beautiful cake and they all joined in an off-key version of the traditional birthday song.

Carrie couldn't remember the last time she'd had so much fun at a family gathering. Annie had them in stitches as she reminisced about the time that the Hanson brothers found an abandoned nest of baby skunks. Apparently there wasn't enough tomato juice at the Rancher's General Store to get rid of the smell. Annie had made Mike take the boys on a fishing and camping trip for a week to get them out of the house until they stopped smelling so much like skunks.

As the laughter died down, Thad reached over and took her hand in his. "You'll have to forgive my family. But if you'll remember, we did call ourselves the Cougar Mountain Mavericks, and believe me, when we were kids we lived up to the name."

"I think your family is wonderful," she said honestly. "I can't remember the last time I laughed this hard."

"What are these big announcements you told us about?" Blane asked, looking from his mother to his father. "It's not right keeping us in suspense like this."

Levi laughed. "Yeah, somebody better spill it pretty quick or Blane's curiosity is going to be the end of him."

"Bailey and Sean should make their announcement first since it's the reason for our announcement," Annie said, smiling lovingly at her oldest son and daughter-in-law.

Sean grinned from ear to ear. "Bailey, would you like to do the honors?"

Bailey reached over and took hold of her husband's hand. "When I called Mom last week, I told her there was a possibility that Sean and I were going to be adding to the family next spring. The reason Mom and Dad made an unexpected visit is because they wanted to be here to share our joy when we found out for sure."

"We're happy to tell you that you're all going to officially be uncles about the middle of May," Sean added, his grin bright enough to light a good-size city. When he kissed Bailey, it was such a beautiful moment tears filled Carrie's eyes.

The stunned look on the men's faces quickly

turned into absolute elation as they jumped to their feet and came around the table to shake their brother's hand and hug their sister-in-law. "This is going to be one spoiled kid," Blane said, laughing. "And I'm happy to say, I'm more than ready to do my part."

"There hasn't been a baby on Cougar Mountain since I was born thirty-one years ago," Thad said, his voice filled with awe. Turning to their mother and father, he asked, "What's yours and Dad's announcement?"

"Arizona is nice, but Wyoming will always be home," Mike said, smiling. "Now that our first grandbaby is on the way, we intend to move back to the mountain so we can be here to see the little guy—"

"Or girl," Annie interjected with an indulgent smile.

Laughing, the Hanson patriarch leaned over to kiss his wife's cheek. "Or girl—grow up. We're going to sell our place in Phoenix. In the spring, we'll start building a log home up at the site where the old hunting lodge stood."

"And we'll be available to babysit whenever his or her parents need a date night," Annie added. "I've been waiting thirty-six years to be a grandmother. I'm not missing a single opportunity to play with my grandchildren."

Blane frowned. "Grandchildren?"

"I'm counting on *all* of you to add to my joy," Annie said, patting her son's cheek. "And that includes you, Blane."

Blane almost choked on his piece of cake. "Aw, Mom…"

As Carrie watched the entire family rejoice in the news of a new baby and the return of their parents to the mountain, she was filled with envy. Glancing over at Thad she knew that one day he would find someone he loved. She would join him on Cougar Mountain to raise a beautiful family and live a wonderful life. The fact that Carrie herself wouldn't be that someone made her acutely aware of the loneliness she'd tried to ignore for the past several years. She'd told herself she was better off without having a special man in her life, but the truth of the matter was, she had been afraid to love, afraid to give someone the power to shatter her trust and self-esteem all over again.

But somehow that hadn't seemed to matter where Thad was concerned. He'd turned out to be the kind of man she'd always dreamed of loving, back when she let herself dream about such things. He was kind, gentle and protective without being domineering. He was loving and loyal to his wonderful family, had dedicated his life to caring for and protecting all kinds of animals and had a deep abiding faith in God. And he'd captured her heart before she'd even realized it was happening.

Her breath caught as the realization settled in that she'd fallen in love with Thad Hanson. As much as she wanted to deny it, as frightening as it was to feel deeply for a man again, she knew it was true. He'd done so much for her. Numerous times he'd saved her life at the risk of his own, opened his home to her for a haven of protection and safety, showed compassion and understanding for her paralyzing claustrophobia and the PTSD she sometimes still suffered, and encouraged and supported her when she tried to conquer those fears. And what had she done for him in return? She'd landed him in danger more times than she cared to count, endangered his family and disturbed the peace and tranquility of their beautiful mountain. Because of her, Thad had been shot at several times, in addition to suffering a concussion and a nasty laceration on his head in what could have been a fatal truck crash.

Carrie took a deep breath as she watched him and his family interact. She couldn't, in good conscience, continue to stay on the ranch, putting the man she loved with all her heart in danger, the only man outside of her family who had shown her that she was worthy of being treated with kindness and respect. If she left the mountain, the danger would go with her. That was what she needed to happen…even if it wasn't what she wanted. She'd like nothing more than to stay and see where their friendship led them. But she'd never forgive herself if she stayed and something terrible happened to him. First thing in the morning, she'd find someone to drive her to the airport in Cheyenne. She'd go stay with her parents and as difficult as it would be to do it, leave Thad behind for good.

FOURTEEN

"The WGFD officer from over in the Laramie region just brought in a cougar that's pretty banged up," Henry said without a greeting when Thad answered his phone the morning after the impromptu celebratory supper. "I think you better come take a look at it real quick-like. It's bad enough I'm not sure whether there's anything we'll be able to do for it. You may have to put it down."

"I'll be right there," Thad said, walking straight to the sink to pour his full cup of coffee down the drain. Trotting across the great room to his office, he reached for a piece of paper to leave Carrie a note, letting her know that he would be up at the center. He didn't like the idea of leaving her alone, but there was an animal in need and she should be safe here. He had three armed men posted around the house and ranch yard. And at his suggestion, she always locked her bedroom door. She had her gun with her at all times and Wilford hadn't shown up for the past several days.

"Thad, we need to talk," Carrie said, entering the office.

"Good, you're up. I need to talk to you, too. I was just getting ready to leave a note, telling you that I have to go up to the rehab center. An injured cougar was brought to the center this morning and I have to take a look at it immediately." He tossed the pen on top of the note he'd started. "Would you like to go up there with me to see what we can do for it?"

She looked uncertain for a moment before she nodded decisively. "I'd love to see you in action again."

"Henry always has coffee made. You can grab a cup when we get up there," he suggested, walking toward the door. He took hold of her hand, and they hurried out to climb into the cab of the rental truck his insurance company had arranged for him to use after the wreck. "You should prepare yourself for it being pretty rough," he warned. "When Henry called he said he wasn't sure if we could save it."

He hoped there was something that could

be done for the big cat. There was nothing he hated more than finding it was too late, that there were no tricks he could pull out of his treatment bag that would make a difference. Too many times, he'd had to give the shots that no veterinarian ever wanted to administer to end an animal's suffering.

"I hope it's not a female," Carrie said as he steered the truck up the narrow lane to the compound. "If she's had cubs this year they won't be able to survive without her."

He nodded. "That's one of my concerns, along with the age of the animal. If it's young and female, losing her might mean as many as twenty cubs that won't be born over the course of the next ten years. If we lose too many females, the species might end up in trouble again."

She nodded. "They aren't on the endangered species list at the moment, but they aren't exactly off of it, either. Cougars are still classified as animals 'of least concern,' but at least that's an improvement from being classified as 'near threatened' like they used to be."

When they reached the top of the lane, Thad steered past the office and drove straight up to the predator building, where

Henry stood by the door waiting for them. "Is the cat still alive?" Thad asked as he jumped out of the driver's seat and grabbed his vet bag from the back seat of the truck.

"She was when I stepped out here to wait for you, but I wouldn't give you a plug nickel for her making it another hour." Henry's shoulders slumped. "I'm pretty sure her back is broke and her skull is fractured. Last I checked, she's still knocked out."

"So it's a female?" Carrie asked as they walked into the building and headed straight for the treatment room. "Can you tell if she has cubs?"

"She's too young." Henry shook his head as they walked up to the stainless steel examination table. "I'd judge her to be a year and a half at the most. They don't start mating until they're around two."

Thad listened to the cougar's heart with his stethoscope, his hopes sinking. "There's nothing I can do for her. She's already gone." This was the worst part of his job. Losing an animal, whether it was wild or someone's beloved pet, was never easy and left him feeling as if he'd somehow failed, even though he knew there was nothing he could have done for her.

"Walt Morrison said they're pretty sure she got hit by a car," Henry said in a hushed tone. "It would have been more humane if it had killed her outright."

Thad knew Henry was grieving the loss of life just as much as he was. "Even if she'd been brought in earlier, I don't think it would have made a difference," he stated, running his hands over the animal's back and skull to confirm his suspicions. "Her injuries were too extensive. I'm sure we'd have had to put her down. The break in her back would have left her paralyzed from the midsection down."

With a couple of suspicious sniffs, Henry took his bandana handkerchief from the hip pocket of his jeans and started toward the door. "I'm…uh, gonna be in…the raptor house if you need me," he said, his voice hoarse. "I'll call the director of the pet crematorium to come and get her."

As Henry walked out of the room, Thad looked up to find Carrie wiping tears from her cheeks. Reaching over, he took her into his arms and held her close. He was feeling the same keen sense of helplessness that he saw reflected in her eyes. "She's no longer in pain," he reminded her, whispering the words against her silky hair. The scent of her herbal shampoo surrounded him and a steely determination filled every fiber of his being. After all the craziness of the past week and a half came to an end he was going to try to pursue a relationship with her.

"When you lose…an animal, do you always…have it cremated?" she asked.

Clearing a lump the size of his fist from his throat, he nodded. "When we get the ashes back we always have a little ceremony with the volunteers and whoever else wants to attend, then we release them in an area of Cougar Mountain where that animal might have made their home."

"I love that idea," she said, her voice no more than a whisper. "It commemorates her freedom of being born and living her life in the wild."

Before he could tell her what her understanding meant to him, his phone rang. "Thad, I need you in the raptor building," Henry stated flatly, then ended the call without any further explanation.

"Something's wrong with one of the raptors," he said, frowning. Henry had always been a man who believed in getting right to the point, but the call was unusually abrupt even for him—and it wasn't like him not to say what was wrong with the animal in question so Thad could start considering what treatment would be needed. Stepping away from her, he took her hand in his and kissed the back of it. "Let's go see what's gone sideways this time."

"Let me know when you have the ceremony to release the cougar's ashes," she said, when he held the door for her to get into the truck. "I'd really like to attend."

"I'd like for you to be here," he said, sliding in behind the steering wheel. There was no doubt about it, she felt as deeply for animals as he did. If he hadn't already fallen in love with her, he definitely would have lost his heart to her today.

When he parked, Carrie was out of the truck before he had a chance to open the door for her. "I hope we're not too late for this animal," she said, meeting him in front of the truck.

"Henry didn't say what was wrong, but judging from his tone, it didn't sound good." He heard the frantic sound of Max barking, which ratcheted his unease up several notches. Max was not a dog who barked all that often. Something was definitely wrong.

He opened the door, but instead of waiting for Carrie to precede him, he stepped in the opening ahead of her. When he walked past the aviary where birds of prey were re-habbed for flight, he noticed the outer door was slightly ajar. He wasn't overly concerned about the birds flying out because they had a two-door system to make sure the birds didn't escape. But before he could pull the door shut and continue on into the office, Carrie pushed past him and let loose a horrified gasp. Rush-ing to see what was wrong, he found Henry on the floor in a pool of blood. The pool was spilling from a deep cut on the side of his head. An agitated Max was pacing back and forth from Henry to bark at the storage door at the back of the room.

In search of a pulse, Thad placed his fingers along the old man's neck. To his relief, the beats were weak but steady. Henry was obvi-ously unconscious. "Call Levi, then dial 9-1-1," he said to Carrie, rising to his feet to grab a roll of papers towels from the storage area. "He's off duty and can get here and start treat-ment faster than the Eagle Fork ambulance."

"Don't either of you make a move toward that phone or your cells. Do it and I'll blow you into the next county," a man commanded, stepping out of the storage room.

Raising his hands to show his cooperation, Thad looked at the man—boy, really—who held a rifle pointed at his chest. "Can we talk about this, Milo?" he asked, recognizing the guy he'd seen at Whisper Lake and then again on the security video.

Without warning there was a loud bang, accompanied by the feeling that he'd been hit in his midsection by a charging bull. The air seemed to whoosh from his lungs and, as if in slow motion, he felt himself falling to the floor. Darkness immediately began closing in around him. He struggled to stay within the light, but his strength seemed to be draining from his body, replaced by a burning sensation in his abdomen that became more intense with every beat of his heart.

He heard Carrie scream, but the sound was fading as he felt himself being pulled deeper into the darkness. His last thought was how much he loved her as he lost his battle with the consuming blackness and slipped into the peace of unconsciousness.

Carrie forced herself to stop screaming and start acting as she shrugged out of her insulated vest, scrambling to Thad's side. But before she could apply pressure to the gunshot wound to try to stop the blood rapidly soaking his shirt, Milo grabbed her by her ponytail and yanked her to her feet, causing Max to growl and position himself protectively between Milo and the area where Thad and Henry lay.

"Don't waste your time worrying about Hanson," he snarled. "He's gonna die and there's nothing you can do to stop it."

Dear Lord, please help Thad and keep him safe in Your care. His only sin has been trying to help me. If someone has to die today, please save him and take me.

Tears ran down her cheeks, but not from the painful hold Milo had on her hair. She'd never been more afraid than at that moment, but the fear wasn't for herself. It was for Thad. He had become as important to her as the air she breathed, and she hadn't had the chance to tell him how much she loved him.

"Why, Milo? What happened to you? Why are you doing this?"

He jerked her toward the door. "Don't act like you don't know. Now, shut up and get outside."

Carrie knew as surely as she knew the sky was blue that if she walked out of the building with him she was going to die. But how could she avoid it? Whether it was due to an over-abundance of adrenaline flowing through his veins, the seething rage that caused blotches of red and purple to mottle his cheeks, some kind of chemical enhancement or the madness that had taken over his mind, Milo Wilford had an almost superhuman strength that she knew for certain she couldn't match. The only way she had any chance of getting away from him would be if he turned her loose.

Forcing herself to remain calm and review her options, she fell back on the self-defense training her parents had insisted she take after surviving Milo's brother. She suddenly stopped dead in her tracks, stomped as hard as she could on his instep, then whirled around and kneed him where it hurt a man the most. He immediately dropped his tight hold on her ponytail and groaned like a dying animal as he doubled over in pain.

Seizing the opportunity to make her escape, she ducked into the flight room she had been told was used to strengthen the wings of rehabbing eagles, hawks and owls. "Now what?" she wondered aloud. She did have the presence of mind to pull her gun from the holster on her belt. But her service Glock was no match for his Remington rifle with a scope and she wasn't sure she could bring herself to aim for center mass with the intent to kill. Going for a more minor injury could make her situation worse, given that her hands were trembling so badly. There was a much greater chance that she'd miss her shot or that the injury would be too minor to slow Milo down. She'd need him standing still and in fairly close range to be confident taking that kind of shot.

She looked around. There weren't a lot of places to hide in the high-ceilinged, cavernous room and no time to give it any thought. Sprinting to the other end, she noticed a space between the trunk of a large dead tree that had been left in the space for a perch and the back wall of the structure. An owl and two golden eagles were perched in the top branches, curiously looking down at her, but she tried to ignore them. She knew that raptors rarely attacked humans unless they were defending their nests or what they considered to be their territory. But they all had talons that could shred things as efficiently as straight razors, as well as beaks that could tear flesh like it was made of tissue paper. The last thing she wanted to do was upset them and put that "rarely attack" theory to the test. She'd always respected their power and hoped they didn't view her as a threat— or a potential meal.

Quickly wedging herself between the tree and the metal wall, she hoped Milo had been too distracted by the pain that doubled him over to notice where she'd gone. Maybe he would think she'd run outside and would search for her somewhere within the rehab compound. But she'd barely finished the thought when the inner door slammed open and Milo stormed into the room. The owl hooted at the sound and the golden eagles turned to glare at the intruder who had dared to disturb the peace of their inner sanctum.

"Where are you, Caldwell?" he shouted.

If he thought she was going to answer him, he was sadly mistaken. She would definitely rather take her chances with three fierce raptors than try to deal with an extremely angry, clearly disturbed man who wanted nothing more than to kill her.

When he walked farther into the flight room, Carrie's heart thumped harder and faster than she ever would have thought possible. She wanted him to leave so she could get back to Thad and call someone to help him and Henry, but after the determination he'd shown, she had little hope that he'd leave any time soon.

"Come on, Carrie, you know you deserve to die." Milo sounded more like a wild animal than a man with his hate-roughened voice. "You're the reason my brother died in prison. It's only fair that you die, too." When he moved a bit closer and stood in the center of the room, she tried to make herself as small of a target as possible and hoped with all her heart the tree was wide enough to shield her from the rifle slugs if he spotted her and started shooting.

"There you are," he snarled, looking right at her. His eyes could only be described as wild, and she wasn't even sure she would have recognized him if she hadn't already known it was him.

"Milo, I didn't kill your brother," she said, hoping to reason with him, but fearing it wasn't possible. "Chip went to prison because he had a terrible temper that he couldn't control. He tried to kill me and..."

"I'm going to finish the job for him," Milo screamed, raising his rifle to his shoulder.

"Milo, listen to me. You don't want to do this. We were always friends."

"Not after you killed my brother," he yelled.

"I didn't kill your brother. He tried to kill me and was sent to prison for that," she repeated.

"He'd still be alive if you had died."

"If he'd killed me, he would have been arrested for murder rather than attempted murder. He still would have gone to prison and for much longer. His actions were his responsibility. They don't make me guilty of killing him," she said, trying to keep her voice calm. "He died because he challenged another inmate and the man stabbed him. That wasn't my fault."

"Shut up!" He ran an agitated hand over his face and shook his head. "You've gotta die!"

"Milo, me dying won't bring Chip back," she insisted. "It will just send you to prison and ruin your life. I don't want to see that happen." He would no doubt have to pay for the crimes he'd committed, but he was so irrational she was hoping he wouldn't realize how steep the consequences would already be. She wanted to keep him relatively calm— or at least keep him talking long enough for help to arrive.

"Tough!" he yelled as he pulled the rifle's trigger.

The loud sound reverberated around the

large, open area at the same time the slug slammed into the tree trunk, sending pieces of bark and wood flying around her in all directions. Startled by the sound and the vibration traveling through the branches of the tree, the big birds perched above her head took flight. The owl and one of the eagles flew to the small ledges in the corners up by the rafters, while the other eagle flew directly at Milo.

As the eagle swooped down toward his head, Carrie took advantage of the distraction the bird provided and fired her Glock at Milo's leg. With a howl of pain, he crumpled to the dirt floor, but instead of staying down as she'd hoped, he managed to ignore the gunshot to his thigh and struggled back to his feet. When he fired the rifle again, she knew there was no way he'd give up until one of them was dead.

Closing her eyes, she waited for him to fire again. *Please, Lord, make him stop before I have to shoot him again or he kills me.*

The sound of a second rifle going off had her opening her eyes. As she watched, Milo fell to the flight room floor. And this time, he didn't get up.

But Carrie could barely focus on Milo.

All her attention was pinned to Thad leaning heavily against the door. He began to sway just before he dropped his rifle, and she rushed toward him. She wrapped her arms around his shoulders as he sank to his knees and passed out. Struggling to keep him from falling face-first onto the floor, she eased him to his back.

"Stay with me, Thad," she said, finally managing to get her cell phone from her vest pocket to dial his brother Levi. Quickly explaining what had happened, she felt only slightly better by his brother's assurance that help was on the way. "Thad, you can't leave me. I love you, and I don't want to go through life without you. Please don't go."

Tears ran unchecked down her cheeks as she held his unconscious body to her. *Dear Lord, please don't let his wound be as bad as it looks. Please let the help he needs get here in time to save him.*

FIFTEEN

Even before Thad opened his eyes, he was acutely aware of the pain in his abdomen and the right side of his back, as well as a beeping noise coming from somewhere beside him. His eyelids felt as heavy as if they were made of lead, and it took almost more effort than it was worth to open them. When the annoying sound became more than he could ignore, he opened his eyes to find himself in an uncomfortable bed in a dimly lit room. It didn't take long to realize he was in the hospital.

He noticed Carrie sat in a chair that had been pulled up close to the bed. Her head rested on her crossed arms on the side of the mattress, and she appeared to be fast asleep. Reaching out, he placed his hand on her silky blond hair to make sure she was really real and not a hallucination induced by pain medication or wishful thoughts.

When she stirred and raised her head, tears filled her eyes and ran down her cheeks. "Y-you're…finally awake," she sobbed, sitting up. "I w-was…so afraid you wouldn't…w-wake up."

"What time is it?" he asked.

"It's just after midnight." She took a tissue from the box on the bedside table to wipe her eyes. "By the time the ambulance arrived, Levi had started an IV and had you ready for immediate transport to the hospital. He stayed with you all the way to the surgery doors."

"Is Henry okay?" he asked, praying the old man hadn't suffered a serious injury.

"He had to have a few stitches and suffered a mild concussion," she said, sniffing. "They kept him here overnight for observation, but he woke up long before you did. He should go home in the morning. He's just up the hall. Your family is down in the waiting room."

Thad nodded and attempted to smile but he was pretty sure it looked more like a grimace. "Did you come here with my family?"

"Yes, your mom and dad insisted that I ride with them. I swear Mike could have won the Indy 500," she said, her mouth curved up into a small smile. "I was afraid to look at the speedometer, figuring I was better off not knowing, but I can tell you, we never lost sight of the ambulance on the way here." She must have noticed it was becoming hard for him to hold his eyes open. "Are you feeling all right?"

"I'm not going to lie, I hurt, but as long as you're okay, so am I." He tried to sit up so he could keep from going to sleep, but a sharp pain sliced through him from his belly to his back, and he sank back against the mattress with a loud groan.

"Please, don't move," she begged, rising from the chair to lean closer. "I don't think the surgeon wants you sitting up until morning." The machine keeping track of his heart rate and other vital signs beeped faster when she brushed his cheek with her soft lips and took his hand in both of hers. "He said you were really fortunate that the bullet didn't pierce any organs. It passed through your abdomen and came out your back with minimal damage, but they did have to remove a sliver of bone where it nicked one of your bottom ribs." She caressed his hand. "You've been through a lot and really need to rest."

He nodded as sleep tried to pull him back into the peaceful darkness. But there was one question he needed answered first. "Is Wilford…still alive?"

"Yes." Her soft hand brushed his hair from his brow. "He made it through surgery, and the doctor expects him to make a full recovery."

"Thank You… Lord," he whispered. He hadn't wanted to kill the boy, but he hadn't been given a choice other than to shoot. When it came to Carrie's safety, he'd do it again if he had to. Feeling truly blessed that he'd protected her and hadn't been forced to take Milo Wilford's life to do it, he gave in to his body's demand for sleep and closed his eyes.

When he opened them again, sunlight streamed into the room through the two windows that looked out onto the hospital parking lot. Spotting his mom and dad sitting across the room quietly talking, he asked, "Where's Carrie?"

"Blane took her to Eagle Fork City Hall to meet with the DCI and WGFD investigators to give her statements. After that, they were going to your place for her to shower and change clothes," his dad answered.

"They should be back anytime now," Annie added, walking over to the bed. She reached down to take his hand, as if touching him assured her he really was going to be all right. "How are you feeling, honey?"

"I've felt better," Thad admitted, using the controls to raise the head of the bed until he was at a more comfortable angle. His stomach and back weren't hurting as much as they had been when he'd woken up earlier, but being shot certainly wasn't something he wanted to add to his list of things to do again. "Has the doctor come in yet? I'd like to find out when he thinks I can be discharged."

"Don't rush it, Thad," she said softly. "Your body has been traumatized, and you don't want to cause yourself to have a setback."

"Don't worry so much, Mom. I promise I'll be fine."

"Hey, Dolittle, it's good to see you looking more like you're going to stay in the land of the living," Blane said, entering the room.

"Where's Carrie?" he demanded, earning a wicked grin from his brother.

"We were stopped by Wilford's brother, Steve, on the way up here," Blane answered. "He told us Milo is facing two counts of attempted murder, assault for knocking Henry upside the head, destruction of state property and whatever else the DA thinks he can charge him with."

"And you left her alone with a Wilford?" Staring daggers at his boneheaded brother, Thad started to throw back the covers to get up from the bed. "How could you leave her alone with—"

"Whoa! Take it easy there, little brother," Blane said, placing his hands on Thad's shoulders to push him back against the mattress. "It's all good. I didn't leave her alone with him. She's just down the hall in the ladies' room, taking a minute to freshen up and pull herself together. The conversation hit her pretty hard. The guy apologized all over the place for what his brother had done. He told us that Milo had started taking drugs after their brother was killed in prison. The family had sent him to rehab to try and get him back on track, but apparently he met some people there who were involved in some kind of cult. He joined up with them after he got out and they stoked his anger over his brother Chip's death. Carrie accepted his apology—but then said she needed a minute in the ladies' room."

Relief as well as shame washed over him. "Sorry," he apologized. "It's just that she's been through more than enough from that family, and I don't want her having to deal with anything else from them."

His brother stared at him until Thad felt the urge to squirm. "You really have it bad, don't you, Dolittle?" Blane finally asked, laughing. "You're sweet on the lady game warden, and I'm just wondering when you're going to tell her. You know it's high time you own up to it, right?"

"Don't start..."

"Save it, little brother." Blane's expression turned serious. "You deserve to be happy."

Before Thad could think of something to say, Carrie walked through the door. At the sight of her, he felt his chest swell with more emotion than he would have thought he was capable of. He was looking at the woman he wanted to build a life with, start a family with and spend the rest of his days doing everything he possibly could to make her happy.

His mom gave him an encouraging smile, then looped one arm through his dad's and the other arm through Blane's. "Why don't we walk down to the cafeteria and get a cup of coffee so these two can talk?"

As Thad watched his parents and brother leave the hospital room, he knew they were right. The time had come to find out if what he heard just before he lost consciousness in the flight room had been real or if he'd dreamed it.

"Did you mean what you said yesterday?" he asked when Carrie walked up to the side of the bed. "Do you really love me?"

Carrie's heart stalled. "You heard that?"

He nodded and took her by the hand, pulling her down to sit on the side of the bed next to him. "It was the last thing I heard before I lost consciousness."

She stared at their entwined hands for several long moments before she looked up to meet his steady gaze. "Yes, I meant it. But I don't expect you to feel the same for me." She smiled sadly. "Nobody wants someone as broken as I am."

He shook head. "You might have been badly bent by your experience with Chip Wilford, but you weren't broken. You survived and that speaks a lot to your strength and the depth of your courage. What happened to you wasn't your fault, but you stood up and saw that he was brought to justice for his crime. I'm sure that was one of the hardest things you've ever had to do, but you did it. That's not something a broken woman could do, sweetheart." He pulled her forward and kissed her so tenderly she thought she might melt. "Now, as long as we're talking about shortcomings, I have a few things to tell you about me," he said seriously. "Things that you might decide are deal breakers."

She had no idea what he could be talking about. She'd seen him in some of the worst situations imaginable, and he'd conducted himself with courage, integrity and a self-lessness that was breathtaking and extremely rare.

"I have no idea what you could possibly say that would make a difference in how I feel about you," she said, wondering if he was having second thoughts about *her*.

"Carrie, I don't exactly have a good track record with dating," he said, the light in his warm brown eyes dimming to resignation. "From the time I learned that girls were about the sweetest things ever, I discovered when I'm around them I turn into a big, awkward doofus. And as my college girlfriend pointed out, no woman wants a man who smells like a barnyard animal and has all the sophistica-tion and finesse of a sloth."

Dumbfounded, all she could do was stare at him. When she finally found her voice, she shook her head. "What in the world was wrong with that woman? One of your most endearing qualities is your love and respect for animals. Anyone who's seen you treat one will tell you that you have a rare and precious gift. You're gentle and kind, and animals respond to you with a trust that is nothing short of amazing. And I've never seen you display anything but impeccable manners."

"But there are times that I misread a situation or open my mouth and stick my foot in it," he insisted. He shook his head. "I'm probably always going to be *that guy* who says the wrong thing at the wrong time when he should have kept his mouth shut."

Cupping his lean cheek with her palm, she couldn't believe how much she loved him. "That just makes you human, Thad. We all have times when we misread a situation and say something we should have kept to ourselves. And just for the record, I think sloths are cute and lovable looking."

Leaning forward, she kissed him—and when he deepened the kiss, she felt as if her heart had finally been set free. But she hadn't heard him tell her how he felt.

When she pulled back to gaze up at him, the look on his face stole her breath and told her all she needed to know. Still, it was nice to hear the words when he hugged her close and whispered into her ear, "Carrie, I'm pretty sure I fell in love with you that first day up at Whisper Lake, when I helped you to your feet after I shot down the drone."

"So where do we go from here?" she asked, feeling a bit unsure. "I haven't been in a relationship in over seven years."

"Me, neither, but I think I know how we should start." He grinned. "I'm not sure when I'll get out of here, but when I do and I feel like I haven't been hit by a bus, would you like to go out to supper and a movie?"

Her heart soared. "I would like that, Thad. I'd like that very much."

EPILOGUE

When he and Carrie arrived at Sean and Bailey's place for the usual Hanson family Sunday supper, Thad steered his truck into the spot between his mom and dad's truck and Levi's. Turning to Carrie, he smiled. "Looks like the gang's all here. Ready to get the party started?"

He'd told her their usual Sunday night supper was actually a party tonight for them to celebrate her not having to testify against Milo Wilford. On Friday, he had pleaded guilty to all charges and been sentenced to twenty-five years in prison. His sentence also required him to make restitution to the state for the damages to the Eagle Fork WGFD station, as well as attend the prison's twelve-step program and therapy sessions for as long as he remained in prison.

"Mmm-hmm," she murmured, clearly distracted. "Who does that black sedan belong to?" she asked, frowning. "My parents have a car that looks just like it."

He quickly got out of the truck to walk around and open the passenger door for her. "I'm pretty sure Chevy has made more than one black Malibu, sweetheart." As they walked up the steps and started through the back door, he stopped to kiss her. "Maybe someone invited guests."

"Ooh, maybe Blane or Levi brought a date," she suggested, looking excited by the prospect.

Thad laughed. "If either one of them did meet someone they wanted to date, Sunday supper would be the last place they would bring her. Bailey told you what a hard time we all gave Sean once we found out he was sweet on her, and you know they needled me pretty good before we actually started dating. What do you think we'd do to them?"

"Good point," she agreed, laughing.

As they walked into the kitchen, they saw Bailey whirling around like a little toy top, checking pots on the stove and a pan of homemade yeast rolls in one of the double ovens and a roast in the other. Pregnancy hadn't slowed her down one bit, even though she was now less than a month away from her due date.

"Do you need help?" Carrie asked.

Thad's sister-in-law stopped looking under pot lids long enough to hug her. "Thank you, but I've got all the help I need. The closer I get to my due date, the more my husband hovers. Lately, Sean hasn't left my side. And as long as he insists on being my shadow, I thought I'd put him to work as my sous-chef."

Sean grinned and waved from the other side of the kitchen as he lifted a large roasting pan out of the oven. "Everyone is in the living room," he said, setting the pan on hot pads on the counter. "Go on in and visit for a while."

"Supper will be ready in about twenty minutes," Bailey said, turning back to a big pot of green beans.

Continuing on into the great room, Thad knew the minute Carrie spotted her parents chatting with his. "Mom? Dad? What are you...?" She suddenly turned her surprised gaze on him. "You knew about this, didn't you?"

He grinned. "I didn't like the fact that you had to miss going up to Sheridan for your mom's birthday a few weeks ago because of that late-season snowstorm, so I invited them for a little belated birthday celebration here."

When she threw her arms around his neck, he laughed. "I guess this means I got this one right?"

"Absolutely." She smiled up at him. "Thank you, so much. It was really thoughtful, and I couldn't be happier."

"I'm glad."

"We wouldn't have missed it for anything, Care Bear," her dad said in his booming voice.

"I'll be right back," Thad said, walking back to the kitchen to get Sean and Bailey.

When he returned to the great room with his brother and sister-in-law, Carrie was embracing her parents. "I'm so glad you came. Where are you staying? In Cheyenne?"

"No, we'll be staying right here on the mountain," her mother said, happily.

"Annie and Mike have asked us to camp out with them on their new homesite," her father added. "We're really looking forward to seeing more of this mountain you and Thad have told us so much about."

When Thad walked up to the three, it felt like his gut twisted into a tight knot. "Carrie, I think I'd better set the record straight," he said, hoping she didn't mind him putting her on the spot in front of his entire family and her parents when he asked the most important question of his life.

She looked confused. "About what?"

"This really isn't a belated birthday celebration for your mother," he admitted. "I flew up to Sheridan last week and talked to your father. After he gave me his blessing, I invited them down here because I thought you would want them to be here for this." He took a deep breath, and before he lost his nerve, removed a small black velvet box from the front pocket of his jeans and dropped to one knee in front of her. Opening the box to reveal a sparkling, pear-shaped diamond ring, he said, "Carrie Ann Caldwell, I can't promise that I won't sometimes smell like a horse or a wild animal, and there will probably be times you'll think I surely am a backwoods bumpkin. But I give you my word, the one thing you can always count on for the rest of your life is how much I love you. Will you please do me the honor of marrying me?"

She covered her mouth with both hands as tears flowed freely down her cheeks, but she didn't make a sound. His heart stalled and he held his breath as he waited several long seconds for her answer. Had he been wrong about how she felt about him? Had he once again misread the situation and made a fool of himself?

Just when he thought he might pass out from lack of oxygen, she offered her trembling left hand, and in a barely audible, shaky voice, she said, "Yes, Thad! Yes, I can't wait to marry you! I love you so much!"

Without a moment's hesitation, he slid the ring onto the third finger of her left hand, then rose to his feet to take her into his arms. Giving her a kiss that had his family and hers applauding, he hugged the woman he loved with all his heart.

Thank You, Lord, for bringing us together and for healing the pain from our pasts in order for us to build a beautiful future together.

* * * * *

*Don't miss these other books
from Kathie Ridings!*

Wyoming Christmas Peril

Get 3 FREE REWARDS!

We'll send you 2 FREE Books plus a FREE Mystery Gift.

FREE Value Over **$20**

Both the **Love Inspired**® and **Love Inspired**® **Suspense** series feature compelling novels filled with inspirational romance, faith, forgiveness and hope.

HARLEQUIN
PLUS

Try the best multimedia
subscription service for romance
readers like you!

Read, Watch and Play.

Experience the easiest way to get
the romance content you crave.

Start your **FREE TRIAL** at
<u>www.harlequinplus.com/freetrial</u>.